THE LAST FIVE MINUTES OF A STORM

THE LAST FIVE MINUTES OF A STORM

*Edited by Sam Agar,
Paula Dias Garcia and
Marc Clohessy*

LIMERICK

2022

The Last Five Minutes of a Storm
ISBN: 978-1-7391383-0-1
PUBLISHED BY Sans. PRESS
JUNE 2022
Limerick, Republic of Ireland

COVER ARTWORK AND ILLUSTRATIONS by Pedro Vó
LAYOUT & BOOK DESIGN by Paula Dias Garcia
TYPESET in Sabon LT Pro and Novela

EDITORS
Sam Agar, Paula Dias Garcia and Marc Clohessy

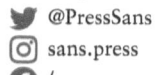

www.sanspress.com
@PressSans
sans.press
/sans.press

The Last Five Minutes of a Storm
receives financial assistance from the Arts Council.

Editor's Note

Paula Dias Garcia

When we asked for stories about storms, we also asked our writers to look at Wallace Stevens' poetry. This may not be an established literary connection, but rather a personal one. Often, I've found myself going back to Stevens, trying to grasp that quiet but elusive quality that seems to permeate his poems – the ability to look upon the world with understanding, to see what is there and accept it.

So when we asked our writers how to find that quality, I was perhaps asking for myself; *how do you see the storms gathering in the horizon and have the certainty that you can make it through once again?* We asked, and our writers told us all about power.

They told us of a power that grasps and holds on with all that its got, but also that knows when to let go. They wrote of power that looks at kindness not as an antagonist, but as an inherent part of itself; of the deep power of being who you are, and of just being, of accepting the universe as it is.

Most of all, they told us how that power isn't really found in the places where we'd expect it to be – and time and time again, it was found inside, and it was rooted in love.

Love for others and for the world, yes, but also a love for yourself, that ran so deep that it simply refused to accept anything less than all that you deserve. It came in wildly different shapes, but consistently the same answer shone through the stories – love that roared at the world and demanded to be heard, demanded all that you truly deserve: freedom, kindness, peace, *greatness*.

In trying to explain all of this, all that we had received from our submitted stories, we found our epigraph, with two quotes taken from almost opposite ends of *Ulysses*. In the beginning, the understanding that the void is unavoidable, that the storms will eventually come; in the end, acceptance, a willingness to be all that you are.

And in the space between those two, the story happens. Between those, *we* happen – and we are so powerful.

The Stories

Content Warnings

*Please beware that discussions of death
and unspecified threat may be present
throughout the book.*

Tin Can Elegy: *Poverty, neglect, violence and injury
involving children.*

tongues/lips/ wrists/teeth: *Sexual trauma* (referenced).

Overspill: *Childbirth/surgery* (recovery), *blood, breastfeeding.*

Tim, the Lantern Holder: *Death (drowning).*

Where the Sun Is Always Setting: *Severe illness, violence, death.*

of wood and stone, and gilded bones: *Warfare, violence, poverty,
death.*

Care Instructions for Your Cryogenically Frozen Mother: *Severe
illness, death of a loved one.*

The Last Airport in America: *Warfare* (aftermath), *injury, death.*

Margins of Snow: *Violent death* (referenced).

Outrunning the Bear: *Unspecified threat.*

One Flap of a Storm Crow's Wings: *Natural disaster* (aftermath),
animal death (referenced), *animal injury, breastfeeding.*

Or Just After: *Natural disaster, domestic abuse* (implied).

*"The void awaits surely
all them that weave
the wind"*

*"yes I said yes I
will Yes"*

James Joyce, ULYSSES

The
November Storm

Chris Bogle

At three minutes past ten, Harry felt lightning strike as a November storm raged outside. A weak blood vessel deep inside of his brain, after waiting seventy years for this moment, finally popped like a cheap birthday balloon. He'd stood up to go to the loo but then toppled, folding to the floor like the air had been let out of him all at once, and he urinated his best grey trousers as he fell. *At least I missed the damned puzzle*, he thought when he came to, looking up at the flimsy foldaway table from his new position on the cracked terracotta tiles. His left side felt as if it had been deboned, like a sleeve without an arm.

Engineering Marvels of the World, the jigsaw was called, five thousand pieces, and there was only one left, a partial picture of a robot neatly oriented with three lugs pointing outwards on the white border of the tablecloth. It had taken Harry two weeks to *nearly* complete it, not because it was particularly difficult – Harry found jigsaws boring and only did it because Jim Scanlon said they warded off dementia – but because the Miniature Steam Railway Committee, of which he was this year's chair, had taken up far too much of his recreational time with their exhaustive prevarications, most recently about whether to update the website. Having eventually made the decision, they'd argued over who exactly should be trusted with the work, how much they should be paid, whether the fee should come from the coffers (versus a fundraising effort) and, crucially, whether including steam-engine schematics might lead to the site being hacked by a *foreign actor*. Scanlon had raised this point last week, setting the deliberations back by a month; having worked for twenty-six years as a technical manager at the waterworks, he considered himself to be a *de facto* authority on critical infrastructure security. Scanlon had had a recent laryngectomy and frequently reminded everyone of his expertise using a speech device that rendered his once sing-song nasality, robotic and monotone. Despite his vocal misfortune Harry had *always* found him insufferable but couldn't say so openly anymore without sounding cruel and unsympathetic.

'Foreign *actors*?', Harry had asked peevishly during the meeting. 'Like *who*? Bela bloody *Lugosi*?'

The committee gasped at his churlishness, and Scanlon huffed and buzzed something about Russian Troll Farms. *Lord help whoever ends up getting that web contract*, Harry thought, although he suspected God would meet most of the committee long before having to help deliver a website.

The vessel in his head slowly doused a lifetime of skills as Harry's world was engulfed in a large swirling blackness that spread from the centre of his vision outwards. His right arm had caught the back of the chair on the way down, sending out a neat hairline fracture across his ulna, and he'd let out a small, creaking *"Oh"*, drowned out by a tea mug that shattered a moment before him in a neat simulacrum of his fate. He noticed as it fell a strange iterating of time, not so much *slow-motion* as a *stop-motion*. Two freeze frames: Before and after, past and future, whole and shattered, the invisible, uni-directional dividing line between, then blackness. He thought about death often, carried it around like a coal sack that could spill its anthracite dust and darken his moods without warning, and he sometimes wondered whether time would stop like a broken projector at the exact moment of his passing, leaving him frozen in the join between two painful thoughts.

Lying down, Harry easily covered the length of his kitchenette, and his feet were wedged awkwardly up against a cheap cream cupboard that hadn't been updated in seventeen years, but which he'd kept perfectly maintained – oiling and occasionally cinching the hinges, shellacking the handles – as he did with everything else in his flat. He was contemptuous of people who bought new things for the sake of it and he believed there was little in the world that couldn't be kept perfectly functional with a bit of occasional elbow grease. He was tall despite his diminishing bones, and even though he'd lost an inch in recent years and tended to stoop, he was still pushing six feet lying flat. His frame had become gangly and had finally relinquished in his late sixties the thick-set strength his body had alloyed from decades in a workshop manhandling metals. The subcutaneous fat in his face had gone, leaving skin that hung slack like a wet sheet over a clotheshorse; his light brown eyes had turned greyish-blue and milky and in place of his beard, sparse white stubble poked through the mottled serrations of his chin in random baby-brush tufts. Harry had never been one for smiling, so instead of deepening laughter lines and crow's feet as it had with James Scanlon, old age had repaid Harry's seventy-three years of stoicism by carving deeper the upturned horseshoe of his mouth, fixing his demeanour like a final engraved portrait. Harry, most people probably agreed, was a miserable coot.

He could see his reflection in the oven door, and he saw to his dismay that his mouth was considerably more down-turned than usual on the left-hand side. His head throbbed excruciatingly in time with the tap that dripped into the kitchen sink and he groaned, partially in pain, but also because he remembered that the tap washer needed replacing and he'd been meant to do it yesterday before becoming distracted. Tomorrow was Monday and the hardware shop didn't open until ten.

Smith had rung at four the previous evening as Harry was writing his to-do list asking – *badgering* – him to see the doctor. It was the third time since Monday, and he was making Harry feel breathless and claustrophobic; sometimes he felt as if he were already nailed inside of a coffin.

'*Leave me in peace!*' he'd growled in exasperation, thumping the receiver down, the bell protesting. But less than five minutes later the phone rang again, and Harry rolled his eyes.

Julian Smith had been Harry's apprentice in the late seventies. He was seen as one of the more talented of the intake – bright, reliable, keen and a whizz with a soldering iron. At sixteen, he had big eyelashes and floppy blonde hair with a nose that was outpacing a face still being moulded by feminine youth. But his soft skin was thick in other ways, and he was completely undaunted by the daily assaults of banter and ribbing. Unlike most of his peers, Smith could tell a level from a grinder and make a decent cup of tea, which put him into the good graces of both lads and management – no mean feat. He'd quickly made his way up the company ladder, bypassing Harry in two years, eventually being sponsored through his degree; Smith loved metal and all the things that could be made with it. Harry had always found him irksome; he was *too* smart for his own good, *too* eager – almost sycophantic and *too* chipper, more concerned with getting on with colleagues than with tight tolerances and diligent work. But Smith always showed a special deference for Harry, even when he eventually became his gaffer. Harry never could put his finger on why the boy took such a shine. Smith would watch him work: measuring, marking and cutting, assembling, screwing, testing, rebuilding; even later, despite his fancy qualifications, Smith would ask Harry's advice, show him his drawings for a technical opinion, and would even ask him over (always unsuccessfully) for dinner. He was in his fifties now, had his own family, his own fabrication company. God only knew why he was still hanging around.

Harry had stared at the ringing phone, the bell hammered and made his head spin, and he waited for what felt like minutes before expelling a loud huff and wrenching it off the hook.

'Was I not clear, Smith, I'm busy in the other room? What's it now?'

'You know you should get a mobile, Aitch,' said Smith, soft Edinburgh still apparent in his voice after all these years. He was winding him up, of course. *Things never ruddy change*, thought Harry, fighting back an urge to smile: *that would just encourage him.* Smith chuckled on the other end, and Harry sat heavily on the old, hinged chair that was kept (oiled and waxed) next to his hand-made telephone table. He'd been having dizzy spells for weeks and he nipped the bridge of his nose, closing his eyes with a sigh.

'Now what would I want one of those for, you foolish boy?'

'Why don't you come over for a bite to eat this evening? Will you come? I could pick you up at six.'

Harry opened his eyes slowly and noticed that the cuckoo clock on the wall needed winding. Maybe the company would be good for him. Maybe a hot dinner was what he needed. He could show Smith the plans for the engine they were restoring at the club and pore over them like they used to, and he could ask Smith what he thought of *his* designs. Maybe he should finally tell him about the will: he'd left everything to Smith, had made it legal twenty years ago. Not that there was much.

'I'm busy this evening, son. Maybe next week.' And he placed the receiver gently back on its cradle as Smith replied, 'Aye. Course,' and asked him again to please see the doctor, before realising that he'd been cut off.

Harry was found by accident and would have passed away quietly like a spent battery there on the cold kitchen floor, with the irregular, metallic *clink* of the galvanised lamppost outside playing a percussive lament to his demise, had old Maud from the upstairs flat not noticed that there were still two pints of semi-skimmed milk on his doorstep. Harry never forgot to bring the milk in, which he knew annoyed Maud, because now she had to steal her milk from two doors down and they had brats who were up before six; they were far more apt to catch her in the act. He was luckier still because she never went out in the rain, not since slipping on the outside stair last year and breaking her nose in the fall. *Won't stop her sticking her beak through her curtains*, Harry had ruminated, but ever since then he'd paid for an extra pint in his subscription, and he'd arranged for it to be delivered to her doorstep. Not that he would ever tell her; he'd never get rid. She reminded him of his mother.

The rain had been hanging in suspension like a prelude to a migraine – somewhere between drizzle and fog – since dawn and looking out over the grim estate in the half-light of this late-autumn morning, Harry mused that the sky seemed to have gone sour and curdled into a scramble of pebble-dashed concrete. The last of the clinging leaves had been torn away and dumped into sodden black-brown drifts along fences, clogging the drains, leaving the trees bare and fractal and vascular. The rain was lashing now. Maud had forgotten to put her lottery numbers on last night, he guessed, and Harry had heard her frantic shuffling as she put on her coat and shoes with the wooden heels long-ago shorn of rubber, then clumped slowly down the stairs clinging onto the railing for dear life, spotty headscarf flapping at full mast. She lived for the lottery, he knew, as if any amount of money could rescue her now.

He'd seen the letterbox flapping and he expected she was having a good nosey, so he wiggled his toes – the only things he *could* still wiggle – and the mad old biddy must've seen it because about twenty minutes later an ambulance arrived, pulling quietly up outside like the volume had been turned down on a monochrome television. By then he couldn't move anything.

'Harry?' she'd squawked. 'You in there, love?'

She used her key and stood to the side of the doorstep, clutching the neck of her Mackintosh against the gnawing wind as the paramedics wheeled him out, and he had seen her surreptitiously pick up the two pints of milk: *waste not, want not*. He could buy more later this afternoon once they'd discharged him.

The ambulance was slow, there was something lazy about the blue lights and the seeming lack of urgency that made people get out of the way quicker, kicking up arcing hisses of spray as they veered onto the hard shoulder, making vehicles on the other carriageway dodge great brown waves, their drivers swearing at the inconvenience. *Bloody ambulances,* a few of them would be thinking. One or two observers crossed themselves, others took deep breaths as they were coercively reminded that after all the busyness, all the fuss, there would be no last gladiatorial showdown for most of them, and the world would probably end in a disappointing abbreviation, an incomplete sentence finished mid-conjunction, in a two-by-three metre box on wheels. Then they turned back into the road and quickly folded those thoughts into one-dimensional origami forms that could be hidden away in a secret drawer and got back to their *important things*.

Somewhere far away, Harry felt someone, presumably a paramedic, take his hand and hold it gently in theirs, whispering, 'It's okay, I've got you.' He wished he could move his lips to tell her he was fine, but something had glued them together and anyway, the last hand he'd held had been his dad's, it reminded him of happiness.

Harry was still clinging on when the ambulance turned off onto the slip road, although by now what little remained of his agency was fading like an unfixed photograph. Hundreds of miles of myelinated fibres and countless billions of synapses curled and withered like burning threads, and the road behind him disappeared into an endless, impenetrable fog. Fields the colour of weak tea segued into clotted rings of semis, and memories flashed as dark blood breached cellular barriers like the flood water outside, sediment solidifying in microscopic cracks rendering the tiny spaces where thoughts lived uninhabitable. The rain had stopped for now and there were fluffy, pinkish vortices appearing in the murk that allowed shafts of straw-tinged sunlight to pierce the churning, lumpen sky with hope of a drier afternoon.

As one of these shafts fell through the window of the ambulance Harry took a few final breaths and froze between two frames. He'd been thinking of his childhood, and the heady rush of steam as he rode the train with his dad. And he also found himself thinking about the day he found his dad, lifeless after his stroke, his mother pounding helplessly on his chest; she went a few months later. Harry was left with Dad's toolkit but none of the tools could fix him. There was no explanation, life just went on: for sixty-three years, fifty days, ten hours, three minutes, and fifty-four seconds.

Back home, Maud was making Harry a milk pudding to eat, for when he felt better; it was her favourite, and a secret recipe to which she had added a tablespoon of Bristol Cream. Smith was wrapping a plated-up Sunday roast – *Mohammed, and the mountain and all that* – and was planning to drop in on the old curmudgeon to make sure he was okay. He was taking his eldest son, Max, to meet him; Max was studying for his engineering chartership and happened to have a special interest in steam engines. The Miniature Steam Railway Committee had placed on their agenda a Sunday evening meeting to decide if the website would benefit from the formation of a subcommittee dedicated *specifically* to its execution, and had despatched the new deputy chair, Jim Scanlon, to go and see Harry and smooth the way. They all arrived within minutes of each other and found Maud tidying Harry's flat, as she had done weekly for years, and they took comfort in talking about steam trains over heaped spoons of milk pudding late into the night. On the way out, Max placed the final piece into Harry's jigsaw and Smith noticed a book with Scanlon's name written on a post-it, in Harry's scrawl, tacked to the corner: *Cybersecurity and Modern Warfare*.

They closed the front door gently behind them and Smith noticed how beautifully easily the hinges swung. Then it started to rain again.

Tin Can Elegy

Tessa Swackhammer

You can't raise a child worth your salt in a tin can. I don't know who said it first, but it was said enough that it became a fact in our town and the next ones over.

This taught me two specific things: I was not shaped like a good child, and my home was shaped like a tin can.

My universe was a donation box in the back of a grocery store, and not the kind that would offer you samples (your hands were too dirty) or had self-checkout lanes (you were liable to steal). Rickety, rusted mobile homes littered the grounds like cigarette ashes on the flat bed of an old, up-turned bucket. We were the bugs circling sucrose in the dirt, ants with big hands trying to carry the load of failures that brought us here in the first place.

It was big enough when I was a girl, because I did not know that there were other buckets, better buckets than mine, that didn't leak when it rained and didn't run red dye into the dirt so much so that it looked like we lived in the back parking lot of a butcher shop. When I was thirteen, I asked for a scimitar as though it was an afterthought when it had been living on the back of my teeth like a peppermint pinched until the meal is over for the last three years. Father, with his bleary eyes and ruddy face folded like a paper bag at the bottom of my knapsack, watched me over the rim of his beer can damp with his spit. *A what?* he'd said, and the anger had been woven in his words like embroidery. *Use your real words, Kid.*

Kid, like a baby goat, like a girl in a tin can with no name because it wasn't worth a moniker, given because the squalling infant wouldn't stop grabbing for it. He doesn't know it, but the nameless version of my name was like a jockey with a riding crop, his heels digging into my hide. I said it louder. *A scimitar is a knife, and I want it*, I said, as though it was non-negotiable. Father does not ask why I want a knife. He says no.

I grow bigger but my universe does not. It is the same incestuous networks of mobile homes grazing in the field like great bison, their rubber feet pawing at the ground, circling each other until the grass turns to wheat beneath the spinning tires. The other children grow warped and twisted like metal sculptures outside the art museum. We are now the bison, and the land is our war grounds. Nobody leaves.

This is the permanency of the tin can life: it gets embedded in your skin like the ticks that live in the tall grass just past your folded out lawn chair. What was once a game: children with knobby knees and bandanas around their heads, wielding broken lumber like swords, becomes something else, like we have chewed and gnashed it into mush, the hard bits of grind crunching against your molars. Why did I need a scimitar? This was a question that had a hundred answers but only two of them mattered, like two copper pennies at the bottom of a ceramic bowl I keep next to my bed. Literal: because it is the best to cut through skin and bone. Theoretical: because it is imperative for someone to be the biggest.

I would like to be the biggest, but everywhere I ask I am told that I will never be – girls cannot take up space the way boys can. *How thin your shoulders are,* they say, slapping me in the centre of my back, *how can you carry the world?*

They walk away as I am screaming: with my hands! with my hands!

I lose the first three fights I am in. The first is a boy with a scar up his lip from the cleft palate surgery his mother paid a doctor in Puerto Rico to fix. *Please*, she'd said, *Fix my son. I can't bear to look at him.* He fights with his knife between his teeth just to show me he has one. He does not take it out – his fists are enough. I lose two teeth, my left canine and my bottom middle. When I look in the mirror, pulling my lip up like it is attached to a fish hook I look like the trailer trash that I am. I am crumpled paper in a wastebasket but one day I will build houses.

My second fight is with a boy that has a name because his parents deemed him worthy. I hate him instantly. His hair is the colour of soot and his body is scrawny and long like the scarecrow in the fields just off the highway pass. I think, there is no way he can win unless he fights dirty, and he does, his hand reaching for the hard pebbles on my chest and driving my face into his knee. This boy is not a nice boy.

I break his bedroom window and pour spiders in from a jar. I knew there was a reason I was getting so good at capturing them, and not just because the screen on our sunroof was loose. It was for this purpose, when I am flat against the siding, ridges of half-made metal tin can against my spine like its own set of vertebrae. The boy screams when he feels the spiders across the close of his eyelids. He will never sleep in the dark again.

Here I learn there are other, dirtier ways to win fights.

The third fight is with a boy with clothes that don't reach his ankles, but is closer, because I have learned from the blood in my mouth from the first two and am fueled by the close circle of youth around this patch of dirt. We feed off of each other like parasites, them drinking our tension like we are the pouches of juice the better kids have at their soccer games, us fueled by the weight of their gaze and the low rumble of appreciation when one of us lands something.

I almost have him, my hands fisting in his hair, bashing his head into the dirt when he flips me over, pinning me back on the ground and for a moment I am frozen again by the weight of his body, the feeling that I am not big at all, that I am nothing but the unstuffed mattress on my cot, springs creaking beneath my weight. I drive my knee into his groin, but it is a futile effort by a girl with no name.

When he cheers, arms above his head, chin tipped up at the sky I look at the long, lean line of his throat with the apple buried beneath the skin and imagine my scimitar chasing the pit.

This is how I know I am not a good Kid.

I sit on the top of the trailer, a cushion ripped from a lazy boy off the side of the road on Mulberry street, where the good houses are, the real houses. Sometimes I close my eyes and I imagine that the cool, crisp wind on my face is an air conditioner in a living room so large I can't touch the ceiling, leaning back on the recliner, cool glass in my hand. I have a mother, and she tells me things like, *girls can be the biggest, Kid* – only my name would be something else, something better – *and you are strong and brave.* In this world, she runs a hand over the length of my hair and tells me that I am already that way and I do not need a scimitar to prove it.

The fights continue, but I stop for a while. I am tired of losing. I look up at the stars and say, *I was not born to be a loser. Why do you keep making this way?* Later, in my bed, I am sleeping and listening to the sounds of my father coughing and hacking outside, my heart kicking in my ribs with the want to be something, anything other than the way that I am. I think the stars tell me to stop pitying myself, but I spit it out into the porcelain shine of the sink and watch the foam go down, bubbling and consuming the grime around the drain hole.

The years stretch and pull on like taffy on the wheel of Duffy's Candy Shop in the window, the joints starting to creak and wane as they try to encompass the more of us, our sour middle-adolescence smell, our trailers stretching to fit our insolence. I have become the essence of a name like Kid – hardly there at all. My father disappears in my fifteenth year, then returns for a week, before he leaves again, his jeans in a puddle by the fridge like he got raptured on his way to get a beer. I step over them for months before rats start to leave droppings in the pant legs and I finally kick them outside.

The fights in the back become a sort of organized blood sport, bets exchanging sweaty palms, the circle in the grass becoming wider, shoes dusted with the orange-red dirt of our butcher shop. I watch from my loser-window like the other loser-fighters in the trailer park that lost and then never got back up again. I do math equations like it is the same as my teeth getting knocked out, my knuckles bloodied, but I am a spitting engine stuck on a carousel, the horses never turning quick enough to burn my energy out.

On a Tuesday – which is important in the sense that it is not important at all, just that I like the word the best out of all the days of the week – I am doing the dishes when the fight moves in front of my window, the two bodies in the dirt perfectly framed by the red shutters I have put on with money I have made at the bottle shop. The one boy is fighting dirty – I think it is the same Soot Boy that goes for the soft buds on your chest and is afraid of the dark and spiders. He is on top of someone. I stop washing to watch, because that is the nature of this, like it is honey and we are flies getting our feet stuck, even when we don't want to watch, we are fascinated with the escalating violence and what it takes from all of us.

I wonder if Soot Boy knows that you are supposed to stop when the other person is down, because the person is down like their body is filled with rice limbs and tied with ribbon, their head lolling as Soot Boy wraps his hands around his skinny neck. The others come racing around the corner like lemmings to a cliff, feet scrambling in the dirt to get a front row seat and I am thinking about public executions, and how they never truly went out of style, they just now happen to kids that live in great metal bison and eat jerky in the wild.

He's going to kill him! someone screams, and they sound abjectly horrified but Soot Boy seems to like it, and I realize in his mind, this is his moment to be the biggest in the yard, that now there is someone that stands at the top of this pedestal and looks down on us like we are worms in fresh, malleable dirt. I plunge my hand into soapy water, my worm-fingers closing around the hilt of the kitchen knife I stole from a diner, one ear cocked for the chaos outside.

Once, when my Father was still trying to be one, he sat me down in the small half-bedroom and told me that being important is about believing that you are, and if you believe anything hard enough, it will begin to exist. I said to him, *you must not have believed in anything, then.* He sat on my bed for a long time after that, staring at the lights outside my small window and the torn blind.

Here, I say to the sharp glint of the blade, I have decided to believe in my own greatness the way I have always thought of it, because I see now that believing and thinking are different things that share a home but never meet. The crowd parts like I am Moses, and these grounds are my Great Sea, and someone says, *who is that?* And they say back, *that's Kid,* with a breath of awe that makes me feel like being Kid isn't that bad, after all – being half-known.

I curl my fingers in Soot Boy's long hair, and now the tendrils are worms, and I am the hawk with talons on his skull, pulling his head back. He swears at me, spittle flying from his mouth like cotton rain. It stops when the knife is pressed to the peach pit of his bobbing throat. *That's enough,* I say, and I am hard and immovable like a stone rolling in front of a cave opening, closing it off from bears and the like. There are two pulse points pounding in two ways: the feather bird-heart of the boy on the ground, the nearly dead, and the boy beneath my knife and his pounding feet on gravel-heart, the nearly dead, but both live.

This is not that kind of story.

The fights finish after that, but the undercurrent of tension remains the same even though it's over, like we're still watching the sky, waiting for the second rush of wind to come through and take the tin roofs off our homes.

There will always be men wishing to be Gods of our playing field, to rule the backs of metal bison, but we understand now in a way we haven't before that it is not our violence that makes us great, it is our decision to show up and be so.

I am not a good Kid, but I am a great one. For now, this matters, because this story will live in half my body like a disease in the blood that everyone will be able to see. It is like the missing canine: the obviousness that I have grown up in a tin can war zone and I have fought and bit my life from the hide until I have earned my fill. One day, this will mean something different elsewhere.

Kid, the stars say, *wake up. There is more conquering to be done.* It sounds a bit like my father, if he were raptured and taken to a place that I cannot see. I wonder if that means he believes in me. I imagine it does. I write it on any space I can find it.

I say, *look at this,* thrusting the knife into the air, the blade cutting through the gusts of wind like muscle and skin.

This is proof that *I exist.*

tongues/lips/
wrists/teeth

Kasandra Ferguson

I've spent about twenty minutes perusing internet search results, attempting to find a detailed description of what a crow's tongue may look like – birds have a variety of tongues, their appearances decided mostly by their diet. The barbed tongues are interesting. I wish I had one, as well as the tiny row of sharp teeth, like geese. I cock my head and stare down the small, circular mirror on my desk, then stick my tongue out. Dismally human, perpetually stained either latte tan or a deep, remnant-Cabernet purple. It feels different today.

I sigh, close my laptop, stare with blackened intent out the tall, rectangular window vomiting eerie light into my long-term residency hostel bedroom. I share it with three other girls, all of us students. A glimpse of Galway sun drifts down into the dead, late-winter grass, and I can feel a smug, misguided charity in it, as if the sky is saying, *Here, take a little*. I know, however, that it is only surface-level warmth, not substantial enough to penetrate the shadows napping between the rows of mossy brick buildings. My mother used to call it 'window weather' – beautiful from behind glass, but upon accepting the invitation to step outside, I would find the light cold and the wind harsh. An illusion. I wonder if the evaporating dew staring through my window thinks the same thing about me.

Accepting the ambiguity of bird tongues, I smudge dark cream eyeshadow over my lids, daub rosy gloss on my lips, and roughly pat my cheeks with matching blush. Black lace drapes my shoulders and torso, a needlessly expensive blouse from my last trip to Dublin, and a leather skirt brushes against my heels. Platform boots and a plethora of rings acting in a dangerous imitation of brass knuckles complete the look.

The familiar mishmash of transient folks bustle around the halls and kitchen, in addition to a dishevelled older woman with crooked teeth and blotchy skin standing shakily by the hot water machine, stirring instant coffee into a to-go cup. I notice James at the desk. He occasionally sneaks homeless people in for a hot drink and reprieve from the rain.

I step out onto the damp sidewalk and feel the first bite of cool air. My nose would be running soon, and my carefully arranged hair would be tangled under the hood of my sweatshirt in less than a minute. A collection of pigeons hop around the edge of the building, pecking at the oats tossed out religiously every morning by a curled-up elderly lady. Above, gulls eye me down, scanning my form for food of some kind. They eventually turn away, disappointed. Last, the blackbirds. They spot the top of stone fences and the corners of roofs. I'm almost afraid to acknowledge their watchful black eyes. They remind me of elementary school teachers waiting by the classroom door, tapping their foot, waiting for me. Always late.

I rush down the cobblestone side streets, hands in my pockets and head turned downward until my neck aches. Bakeries, cafes, music shops, takeout restaurants, salons, pharmacies, knitwear, pubs, pubs, pubs. I round the corner onto the bridge by the Spanish arch. The air is brackish, the river underfoot rumbling slightly. Low tide. I've had little luck interpreting its moods, but some days (particularly in the summer) it ran calm and clear enough for swans to drift by unperturbed, and others (more as of late) it rushed harder than the white water rapids I'd rafted through in the Smoky Mountains on family vacations.

The low lighting and light, burbling conversation across the joint sets me at ease once I pass through the faded double doors of my favourite bar in the West End. My eyes scan the booths and high-tops only briefly before catching my regular crowd tucked away in the corner, already jostling with laughter. I swing by the bar and request a stout before sitting. A strain in my jaw and shoulders I hadn't noticed until now dissipates. I stomp over – everything is a *stomp* in my boots, and I like the presence it gives me, but I wish I was lighter of foot. My mom used to complain about hearing my footsteps across the house. I wish I could hop on talons, carried by a breeze.

'Familiar nonsense?' I ask as I sidle into the booth.

'Get all your work done?' Deborah asks. She has large, curly black hair, sallow skin, and blue eyes, almost grey. I make a face. 'Didn't think so.'

All red hair and freckles, Órla chimes in as she sets her beer back down on its coaster, dabbing creamy foam from the corner of her lips, 'Don't you have an essay due tomorrow? Was it two or three thousand words?'

I grin. 'Three.'

'Oh,' Deborah groans, 'you're going to give *me* stress ulcers.'

'Ach, let her be!' crows Fionn. A lock of his lively hair, cinnamon-brown and begging to be combed through with fingertips in that early-stages Marlon Brando sorta way, bounces against his forehead as he jolts forward, forever seized by whatever claim of passion happens to throw itself through his lips. 'Surely she can let loose a little?'

Órla snickers. 'You have something due tomorrow too, then?'

He shrugs and sniffs. 'Irrelevant.'

A loose smile leans across my mouth, easy and indulgent. My counsellor told me I shouldn't be alone with my thoughts; I need engagement. Stimulation. (Enrichment, like zoo animals.) Friends are good. I stare into my pint. She also diagnosed me as a high-functioning alcoholic.

What's the point of being high-functioning without *the substance abuse? It's called personality*, my brother joked. I take a sip.

We dip and sway through the familiar topics – overbearing professors, absentee professors, upsetting group projects, the horrendous hostel night porter, disappointing disco nights at the local club, the added weight induced by a diet of instant noodles and beer, so on and so forth. Fionn tells me under his breath, across the table from me, that the extra weight could only accentuate the quality of my ass. I will away an incoming blush, white-knuckling the psychological need to resist feeling flattered. We slept together last semester after a wine-driven dance party somewhere in the woods. I couldn't pick out the location of our shindig on a map, though there are a slew of photos and exciting stories to mark the occasion. Some particularly flattering topless pics of me and my friend from Chicago, who has since returned to the states, are the *pièce de résistance* of the evening, along with some torn clothes acting as the laughable reminder of a mostly-mock brawl where we all began wrestling in the shrubbery. Humans' need to touch each other intrigues me, achingly.

There are no remnants of our rushed intimacy, though, except for his occasional whispered comments and a burning memory of a trail of hickeys and bite marks along my tits and the inside flesh of my thighs. We never spoke about it, which I've learned is exceptionally Irish. I wonder if he thinks about it, the feel of me. I think about his teeth. Often. The old saying, about trees and unheard sounds, slithers underneath my thoughts: if an event exists in one person's head, unspoken, unknown by anyone else, did it really happen? Does it really matter?

A hand encloses around my wrist, and I jerk away. I wrap my arms around my centre. Deborah freezes, expression taut.

'Oh, I-I'm sorry, you seemed lost in thought,' she says hesitantly. Órla and Fionn watch me hawkishly, concerned for any sudden storm of tension. 'Are you okay?'

I pause, tongue heavy. A cheaper smile stretches over my face. 'Of course, you just startled me. Thinking about conclusions for that goddamn essay.'

The apprehension drains away. I settle. Underneath the table, I keep rubbing my wrist, chest tight.

'You're so American,' Fionn chuckles. He adopts his most horrible, wooden western accent. '*That* goddamn *essay.*'

'That rootin' tootin' essay,' Deborah adds, lifting her half-empty pint. Órla clinks it with her own, crying, 'That gosh golly darn essay!' Fionn and I quickly swing our own glasses into the cheers, laughing.

I take a swig and slam the glass down. I see strange, black spots sprouting under the skin at the base of my hands, like porcupine spines waiting to protrude. I ignore it. The live music is starting soon.

I cross the narrow, cluttered bridge on the way to university the next day, a hangover rattling dully in my skull, my eyes numbly tracing the outline of the cathedral. I know very little about Catholicism. The aesthetics are enjoyable, but like the native language, many Irish people tell me there's no use learning the inner workings. The entrance of a church always calls to me. Religion is a tangled memory; a church foyer, its free coffee and warm greetings and familiar old-church-carpet-smell, strikes a feeling pleasant and deep. Like roots.

I turn and walk along the river, past a vine-covered stone fence and a cottage framing a cement pathway. Weeds and long, wild grass, still crisp and yellow from the lingering cold, compete for breathing room in a stretch of free space to my left, and birds step comically amongst the jungle, pecking at the dirt for worms.

A fresh, heavy breath of the air sucks past my teeth, and I smile, trying to savour the pre-class freedom. My courses are interesting, motivating even, but in these days when I am forced to rise earlier than I'd naturally be inclined, I always find myself wishing I could flit about as I wanted. There are so many places I want to go.

My eyes slide along the path in front of me, and I pause, foot raised. I'd nearly stepped on something.

Before me is a pair of bird wings, wrenched from their body, the ends of the humerus bones still spattered with blood and torn flesh. They splay outwards, fresh and glistening with the morning damp. No dogs root through the grass around me – many older folks would take their pets along this route for early walks, though I can't imagine the owners allowing their dog to dismember a bird. The rest of the body is nowhere in view. Mouth twisted, I keep walking.

The air is bearing down on me, and I can hear the river over the fence rushing harder than usual: a storm would wander along soon.

Riotous conversation, drinking, dancing, pool-playing, flirting, and swishing, hormone-spiked feelings shake the hostel. It often feels this way on weekends, charged with energy, potential. The churn of old faces and new impart an indescribable, palpable electricity. I have since recognized this, unfamiliar as I am, as fun. Or so the freshman tell me. I enjoy it in a way I didn't used to.

When I was your age, I want to say, but the thought makes my stomach turn. Twenty-four hurts. It is clinging to vivacity, to being called *pretty* instead of *hot*. I pretend not to mind. It's not progressive of me.

The common area is packed to the brim. Girls in ruched dresses and faux-leather jackets combine liquors and mixers that should never touch each other, and a cluster of lads trade jokes over cards and crisps. The nationalities are mingling, accents traded in a lively, anticipatory fashion. I nestle into a chartreuse vinyl chair.

'There she is!' cries Haylee, a cloyingly sweet eighteen-year-old with a curtain of silken brown hair.

I remember doing the same thing as a teenager: befriending the individual with the highest status in the room, lapping at the remnants of social influence like a cat desperately licking the bottom of its bowl for the last bits of cream. I'm not used to being on this end of the relationship – she reminds me of my foster sister. Teetering on the edge of something not yet understood. She's in university now, too, studying Economics.

35

The rabid desperation of Haylee's grip on the concept of Fionn, as well, the headache-inducing floral scent of her youthful crush, is tangible. He's nestled dead between our ages, a fact which haunts me.

'Hey, baby,' I croon. Part of me craves to run a hand over her hair. Instead, I uncork my wine.

A corset-bound classmate of hers named Aoibhinn leans over, green eyes flaming. 'Eileen, solve something for me, would ye?' She jerks her thumb behind her at Oisín. 'If a girl says she likes it rough, does that mean she's automatically got daddy issues?'

'Not *only* daddy issues,' Oisín chimes in. He is a handsome young thing, lean and sculpted, but I can tell his hair will start thinning before he hits thirty. 'But a girl asking to be slapped around definitely means she's got trauma, right? I'm only trying to look out for her.' He puts his hands up. 'Why reinforce that shit?'

The fluorescent lights start to hum louder in my ears like a swarm of bees; the chatter around me chafes against my skin, too loud, too much, too everywhere. I take a breath to calm myself.

'Sometimes,' I respond, gentle, self-assured, nonchalant, and pour my glass. The *glug-glug-glug* makes me think of my mother's laugh. 'People get accustomed to pain.' Oisín gears up for some sort of victorious remark, but I smoothly add, 'But not always. Pain and pleasure enhance each other, like sweet and salty. Some people just catch onto that. No use judging.'

Bodies tense, they watch me, along with Haylee and a couple of their friends. Authority bolsters my tone, and they're so fresh, so hungry to know and feel and be near each other. It is a non-answer, wispy and uncatchable as smoke.

They descend into more nonsense conversation about sex, and I know the night porter will be warily stumbling upon one or two pairs of them entangled messily in the corners or group bathrooms around two in the morning, post-pub crawl. My tongue is sore – from talking? Drinking? I covertly stick my finger in my mouth and trace the side of my tongue, then flinch. The flesh feels raw. Something pokes the top of my finger, and I turned my attention to my teeth. Pause. The edge of my canines seem sharper than normal. My incisors, then my molars: the same. A dentist once told me I have the molars of a caveman, flat and deep-grooved, hence my proclivity for cavities. Now, though, they feel filed down, pointed, sore at the root. I hastily rip my hand away and try to keep my mouth shut.

Fionn, Deborah, and Órla eventually wander back from their liquor run, upon which they no doubt got distracted by some shenanigans with our other group members, Colm (Glasgow transplant Linguistics major), Alice (third-year Donegal Law student), and Freya (Hamburg Erasmus-exchange Physics major).

Fionn slams into the chair next to me with one large hand gripping a honey-flavoured bottle of Tennessee whiskey. 'Felt I'd pay homage to you,' he jokes, shaking it in my face. I give a tight-lipped grin.

'What riveting conversation have we missed?' Colm asks in his bouncing Scottish accent. Something about it always puts me at ease.

'Sex, trauma, and possibly misogynistic stereotypes,' I murmur, barely surmounting the volume of the surrounding conversation.

'Thank God I was late.'

Alice rolls her eyes. 'I'm sure your insight would've been life-changing.'

'The romantic culture of Celtic men,' Órla sighs, and the girls laugh. The boys purse their lips and sink back.

We talk and shout and joke; the boys break off to play pool, and flirtatious girls follow to slink around the table making suggestive comments; I wander out to talk with those craving a smoke break; Deborah breaks out her guitar and starts singing, all hot caramel and smooth brandy voice; I drink and drink and drink into the bottom of my wine bottle. My teeth seem to dull with every glass, returning to their typical shape, and I'm not sure if that makes me happy or not. The black pin-pricks under my skin have faded.

Eventually, someone catches wind of live music at one of the more niche bars in the East End, and the news ripples through the crowd. A mob of people gather, ready to wobble the windy walk over and soak in the last bit of tunes before the bars close for the evening. Fionn is instantly ready. Drinking makes him manic, a trait usually reflected by me, though tonight I am more sombre. I have been all week, but I try to mask it to avoid concern.

Don't think, don't think, don't think about it–

'Are you ready, Eileen?' he interjects into my spiral. I attempt to rally myself. Feet ground into the hideously patterned carpet, I heave myself out of the chair and paste on a grin. He seems on the brink of vibration, so happy and brimming with energy. 'Fuck yes!'

We venture out. Rumbling in the clouds like God clearing his throat is an oncoming storm – I just know. I can practically feel the river bisecting the city whipping itself into a frenzy. The walk is brisk, nearly enough to make me turn back, but I tighten my scarf around my neck and tuck my hands under my arms.

It doesn't take fatally long to find the bar, and music floods the building and spills out the door, riling us all. A mixture of similar young drunks and resident old men take nearly every seat, so we squeeze into the free spaces, stomping our feet and swaying as the band shifts from traditional, folksy songs on their guitars and banjos and *bodhráns* to feral, thumping covers. Tequila shots and dripping lemons are pressed into my hands, and I consume them desperately.

An Arctic Monkeys cover moans into being, and I suddenly remember sitting in a cocktails-and-dumpling joint in the Fremont District of Seattle late at night with my then-roommate and a hostel guy, the kind lingering around the common area seeking a connection. This one had terrible taste in literature. If I remember from his social media feed before I unfollowed him, he ended up in Australia, waving chequered flags at diesel-soaked car races. I've had so many memories surging into the forefront of my mind lately. I feel my teeth poke again, the prickling underneath my skin. Anxiously, I run a hand through my hair, but its texture has changed, ruffled and strange. I grab a piece and rip it out. Mouth agape, my eyes take in its feathered appearance. My dark brown hair has turned nearly black.

My head whips back and forth, afraid to see what people may think, but they're going about their drinking, slurring, dancing. Do they care? Are they too inebriated to notice? Or is the transition simply not as frightening to them as I find it?

You're not as terrible as you think.

An old friend: a communist, Nazi-brawling, beef jerky strip of a man running a crowdfunded organisation aiding the homeless population in northern Seattle. Stabbed four times by twenty, knew how to shoot a semi-automatic by age seven. Prior heroin addict, now married and stable, if not rubbed raw and scraped thin by the bottomless hole of terror in his past. The only man who could listen to my stories settled and calm, making no attempt to console me, ripping apart my relationship with the belief that I am, inherently, barely human.

Maybe you aren't. I'm not. I am what I am. Do you think a vulture doubts its purity because it has a complicated relationship with living things? Do you think snakes and centipedes and those frightening creatures have no purpose? Do you think crows are only omens of death?

No, I'd replied. *But everyone thinks they are. Isn't that enough to damn them?*

They don't have an air of death naturally. They feel and mourn. People are scared of them, I think, because they have long memories. Memories are terrifying things.

I refocus on the feather in my hand. A booming sound shakes the pub, and it jolts me into action. Jittery with liquor, I dip into the booth where our group dumped our coats and rifle around for my jacket and scarf. Frantic energy rattles my limbs. I am shaking like the wind, like the clouds, like the storm outside. Rain begins pattering on the rooftop; tears start gathering in the corners of my eyes to match.

I finally tear my outerwear from the pile and shrug it on as I stomp towards the front door and out into the rain. It's an absolute torrent. Sheets of rain attack the roadways, and I see a variety of late-night drunks crouched in doorways with their waterproof coats' hoods pulled far over their faces. I make no attempt to protect myself. Attempting not to slip on the streams of water pouring over the sidewalks, I dart towards home, shrouded in the hazy grey of the downpour. My hair is soon slicked to my face, droplets of water dripping off my nose. The taste of rainwater is refreshing in my mouth, in a way, chipping away slowly at my drunkenness. I am only a minute or two from the hostel when I hear a muffled cry. I skid to a stop.

'Eileen, you absolute lunatic!' Fionn shouts over the roar of the storm. 'What's possessed you?'

He stops next to me, jacket pulled uselessly over his head. His hair is pasted to his forehead, and his youthful skin is waxen and pale. Guilt seizes me.

'Christ, you didn't have to come after me!' I say.

'How could I not?'

A clarity grips his face, as if there were no other option. I'm not sure what feeling settles in my gut in response to this.

'I just– I needed to be–' I toss my head around, but I fail to find the end of my sentence in the barely-visible crooks of the back road I've run down. 'I'm not well.'

He screws up his lips. If I were to describe perfect lips, I would simply describe his, soaking in the reverent memory of them tracing over my hip bone. The expression crinkles his nose, too, small and just a hint crooked, leaning into the very reasonable assumption that it had been broken. Most likely by somebody else.

Suddenly, he drops his coat onto his shoulders and grabs me by my upper arms. I gasp, and he wrenches me into the nearest doorway. Moody red lighting creeps from inside the frosted glass windows in the door. I hadn't noticed specifically where I was, but we'd ended up just by a late-night coffee-and-wine cafe. I'd been in just once; something about the decor reminded me of the entrance to sex dungeons on the West Coast: soft, suggestive, warm, hushed. Given reprieve from the rain, I see his face more clearly. His brows are knit, his hazel eyes conflicted.

'I know.'

We push into the cafe. The woman at the bar looks disappointed with our state, sopping wet clothes and bedraggled, drunken attitudes, but she tells us to grab any booth. We slip into one with worn benches, a glossy, cherry wood table, and red velvet curtains. An emptied, ancient liquor bottle sits in the centre of the table, corked with a small, scentless candle dripping wax down its dingy surface. A graveyard of burnt-down candle nubs are piled in the bottle's innards, filled with sooty memories of all the conversations that have been held over their wicks. I order a red wine; he orders white. He tells me it's because I'm more mature – I can't handle sweet rieslings or acidic pinot grigios anymore. It's a bit true. I eroded my oesophagus a bit back in the day, always downing a bottle of white before bed. My counsellor said to be watchful. The physical impacts would linger for a long time.

We sip at our glasses in silence for a moment. He's not good at this. Something is hiding behind his teeth, pressing desperately from the inside of his mouth to gain freedom, and it's the same for me.

'I've missed you lately,' he blurts, then blushes. I've only known older men in this sense, and they never blush. The instinct is wrung out of them. Something about the look of it makes my blood sing.

'I've been right here,' I say dryly.

He frowns. 'You haven't been, though. I know you think I don't watch you.' He pauses. 'That sounds creepy. I mean – I pay attention. To you.'

I feel my expression go cold, hesitant. 'Do you?'

'You do the same. To me.'

I swallow. *Don't be a pussy.* 'Yes, I do.'

'We never talk about this. *Us.* I'm sorry. I've never been as open as you, a-as good at this, but–'

'You think I'm good at this?' I say sharply. I wish I could be. Something about his obvious intention to pry, though, sets me on edge, even as I admire the pour of candlelight over his cheekbones.

'Well, now that you say that,' he chuckles and sips his drink. 'But I do miss you. I know something's on your mind. You have no reason to tell me, and no obligation. I *want* to know.' He picks up my hand and squeezes it. I try not to flinch. 'I want to know.'

I sway on the edge of a decision for a moment. Need or desire or tequila makes the choice for me. The storm seems to crescendo, and even the bartender glances up at the ceiling, concerned.

'I-I've had... very old memories resurface. I ran into somebody at a bar last week.' I suck in a breath, then sigh. I can't look Fionn in the eye. 'He looked *so much* like a man I knew when I was a teenager. So much. He called me *baby*. And it's like something slithered out of my guts, into my throat and out my mouth. I'd never had this memory before. But I know it happened to me, and I just– I just don't know what to do with it. It's there now.' The shake shivers back into my body. He holds my hand tighter. The pricks of black are pushing through my skin, bristling into fresh feathers over my hands and arms, dark as an oil slick. He doesn't seem to mind. 'I wish it would crawl back into the hole it came out of, but... but I also want to throw it at everyone. I want to tell somebody, but the idea of what would happen if I did doesn't make me feel good. I'm afraid of what it'll do to me.'

He waits for a long time, using his free hand to drink his wine. There is a glaze over his eyes, but he still seems invested, attentive. Finally, he opens his mouth.

'I think... there is an artistry in knowing where to *put* memories. They're not confetti or currency.' He chews on his lovely bottom lip, thinking. 'You're an artist. A painter and a singer. I admire that. But even you mess things up.' I laugh, tired but earnest. 'I know it's heavy. I know it is. You're so

Atlas, it hurts. Not everybody deserves what's on your mind, but you need to know who to let carry it.' He leans in closer. 'I'd like to.'

I suck in a breath. Something beneath my ribs breaks open, and the ceiling of the cafe matches. The wind tears at the ceiling – I hear a deep, sharp, wrenching noise, and I see gaps beginning to open at the roof's edges. Water spills in and pours down the walls. The bartender startles, but goes back to drying glasses. Fionn is still watching me.

My mouth opens; the sky is placed down. He bears it gracefully. At its end, he runs his hand up my arm, my neck, across my jaw, eyes full of my own grief.

'You're not evil, Eileen.' His hands are soft, warm. 'These things make you into something new, but you're still good this way.'

A craved burning spreads over my skin as I tilt forward and press my mouth to his. The roof has peeled back ever further, and the storm creeps closer to our table, chilling our skin and raising goosebumps. I feel a breaking, reforming at my shoulder blades, then my hips. My wings press at the edge of the table and the inside of the booth, their feathers brushing the curtains. I think of his teeth and his tongue, wishing it was like mine, but enjoying the feeling of it nonetheless. Eventually our mouths are no longer compatible. An ache strikes my jaw, and I pull back out of the booth, rubbing my cheeks as if seized by a toothache. The transformation is painful, jarring, an indescribable slipping around of my skin and muscle. Eventually, a memory of my body slumps to the floor, and I perch on the edge of the table on fresh talons. The new body is lighter. I cock my head at Fionn; he mirrors my position, smiling heavily. With one great, final pull, the roof is ripped from the building, and rain coats us. He picks me up gently and sets me on the bench next to him to keep me dry. We sit contentedly until the rain soon dissipates. Irish weather is changeable.

'Come back when you're ready, okay?' he says in a tone I've never heard from him before, eyes on the sky.

My beak does not allow me to smile, but I believe he feels it. There is a quiet, special nook I have observed many times before next to the river, nestled in between a series of vines and butterfly bushes that would bloom come the end of spring.

Overspill

Aoife Esmonde

The night feeds were the hardest.

The baby was still so small then – not much more than a dense lump of flesh in her arms – and sometimes she thought she was going to go mad from it all. She'd spent so long preparing for the birth, but she hadn't really thought about what it would feel like *after*, when she was alone, lying there as if tethered to the bed, the baby like a hot stone against her straining breastbone, and the mindless, maddening need to feed and feed and feed.

She felt simultaneously empty and bloated, stitches stretched as tight as a drum, with stuff coming out of her for weeks that was hardly blood at all. It was dark and jellyish, and looked like it was supposed to be still inside of her.

On the first night, the baby's eyes stayed closed, though he was awake for hours, mewling for milk and batting at her tender skin with his small square fists. She was thirsty, almost thirstier than she could remember ever feeling, but she couldn't put the baby down without him making that querulous hiccuping sound, and anyway she didn't really want to be away from him for too long.

On the second night, she woke the baby's father and passed the baby over. He took the small body so tenderly and gladly that she almost felt bad, watching him blink into wakefulness and curl into the baby's body with a joy that seemed effortless. She felt a sly sort of shame as she slipped out of the room, and wondered if leaving the baby would always feel like this.

It was quick and simple to take a walk in the hazy grey-edged city night, to get something to drink. It didn't take long, and the relief of it settled in her with something like an ache. But it was too hard being away. She missed the baby shifting on her chest, his chin nudging the bottom of her breast, mouth opening in silent dismay before she slid his mouth onto her nipple. She didn't stay out for long.

He fed and fed, in those early nights, throat working furiously, mouth splayed wide over her areola, the suck and gurgle of his drinking a counterpoint to her heartbeat, the two of them locked together, flesh on flesh. Sometimes it felt as though she would never be enough.

She took the baby out every day, in the pristine new pram that she'd picked out before he was born, back when she could never have imagined the discontented, demanding, infinitely beloved reality of him. He was still all scrunched up, skin crepey and flaking from soaking too long inside her. A lacy spread of rash bloomed along the place where his jawbone was buried under a sweet excess of flesh. Milk spots, the nurse'd told her, a whole constellation of them that she could follow with her fingertips when he lay against her in the dark. He wasn't smooth and flawless and pretty like babies in magazines, but she thought he was all the more charming for it, with his lopsided thin mouth and the heavy hang of his cheeks and his vaguely quizzical expression.

She walked everywhere, pushing the pram ahead of her like a proclamation – *I'm just like you!* – and because the baby slept so much, and the days were short, she didn't have very much else to do except stroll.

The city was so small. She had hated that at first, but now she realised there was something comforting in feeling as though she could take it all on. Some days, she followed the curve of Patrick Street all the way across the river, and then up the big hill, taking the strain from the pram in the back of her thighs, until she reached the wide green space at the top where the whole place was spread out below her; manageable, bite-sized.

Some days, she walked all the way from under the golden fish on Shandon Steeple to under the golden angel on St Fin Barre's, because she liked the cool dark spaces that formed so close to the cathedral walls, and the effortless sag of gravestones. She was always lonely, but she didn't mind it as much there, under the soaring span of the old walls.

Some days, she just walked the river, especially when they went out early, especially if the light was good. There were so many bridges – *Brian Boru, Mary Elmes, Patrick's, Christy Ring, Millennium, North Gate, Vincent's,* and on and on – with the winter sun slicing up the water and the river like a bared throat leading her forwards. No one ever bothered her, and by the time she reached the Mardyke and the bare bleached ribs of the footbridge rose above her, the baby was usually awake. One day she brought a padlock along, with her initial and the baby's scratched into it, and she took the baby into her arms while she clicked it into place on the bridge alongside all the others, knowing it would probably outlast her. She didn't cry, but she felt like she wanted to.

Sometimes, she had to have a drink, though it was trickier during the day. There were always too many people around, and with the pram, it was harder to be quiet, to go unnoticed.

The first time she had a drink when she had the baby with her, he started to cry.

She was already pressed up against the man, latched on tight, mouth wet first with anticipation and then with the fresh salt burst of blood at the first slide of her sharp teeth, too fast and unsubtle with raw hunger.

She sucked a mouthful, then a second and a third, the blood bodywarm and syrupy in the back of her throat. And then she heard it. A murmur, an angry-sounding cough, and then the small squalling sound of the baby wanting something. Out of the corner of her eye, she could see the blanket in the pram writhing where the baby had begun to kick his legs.

The man was leaning against the wall under the Shaky Bridge, eyes closed, breath slowing along with the sluggish beat of his heart. She never took too much these days, just enough to keep her going until the next time, but he should have been out cold already. At the first sound from the pram, the man's eyelids fluttered with a foggy sort of wariness, and when the baby let out a proper cry, the man frowned, tried feebly to turn his head. It was very distracting.

She lay him down on the ground, tucked far away from the edge of the water. Above them, she could hear people jumping on the bridge. 'Still shaky!' they shouted, and then the baby started to scream properly.

It had all been so quick, but by the time she managed to get the brake off the pram and the wheels were churning sluggishly up the ramp to the road, she could feel her bra growing hot with spilled milk.

It felt relentless, this treacherous, uncontrollable response of her body to the baby's needs, but she realised she didn't mind this new sense of her own usefulness. In the park, she found a nice bench right near the children's playground where she could sit and feed the baby. Every part of her felt alive, like her blood was rushing a little too close to the surface of her skin. She wasn't thirsty anymore.

Just as the baby slackened into sleep she saw the man wandering towards the public toilets. He looked confused, and though he walked right past her, he showed no sign of recognising her, or even noticing her at all. The puncture wounds were nearly healed already, she saw with relief. It was good to know that she could still get away with it, if she needed to, though after that she started going out in the evenings instead.

Everything she did was easier in the dark.

Being careful wasn't always enough, though, or maybe it was just that some people could recognise something in her – that *something* that was ancient and weird and made her feel so tired sometimes.

Threading the pram through the rush of bodies out of the North Cathedral after mass one morning, she saw the woman – small, careful eyes, hair a lacquered sheath of curls, good coat, good shoes, good living – and the woman recognised her, or remembered *something* of her anyway. They looked at each other a little helplessly, the woman's eyes sharpening, and then the woman turned to the pram.

'He's handsome, love. He's the image of you.'

She shrugged; she thought the baby was all himself, but she said a nice thank you all the same.

'You're not from around here, love, are you?'

The tone was kind, but the eyes weren't, and when she didn't answer, the woman blessed herself furiously, hand dipping into the holy water font at the cathedral door, and then pulled her hood up and hurried away, face downturned. The Shandon Bells rang out as she watched the woman go, an imperfect tune, and the baby started to cry. She knew she'd have to think seriously about leaving.

She wasn't sure when she first got the idea of bringing the baby with her.

She'd had a baby already, a long time before. That baby, a different little boy, had been small and pale and quiet in the way that some babies are. She had loved him, but maybe she'd been less selfish then, or just less lonely, because she'd left when he was five and she hadn't gone back. It was kinder for everyone, and anyway at the time she didn't think she could bear seeing her little boy grow up and get old. But in any case, it didn't matter anymore. That baby must be long dead by now.

But the new baby was different, somehow, even though she had promised herself right from the start that she'd have to leave him behind too. And she would have to do it soon, before he started to remember her. It would be the right thing, she told herself, to slip away in the night, let him believe she had been just another bad mother, let his lovely dad take care of him and grow older alongside him, like parents are supposed to do.

But once she thought about bringing him with her, she couldn't quite let it go. Sometimes she knew it would be cruel to do it, like when she sang him nursery rhymes and had to put him down so she could be sick in the sink at the line, "pretty maids all in row". It made her remember all the people she had used along the way – their fluttering, frantic hands beating like moth wings against her back as she fed in a frenzy, and their terrified, open, silent mouths, and the relief when they finally went still.

She had thought she was a monster at first, when the thirst was so sharp and cunning and compelling that she would have killed for it. *Did* kill for it. It had taken her ages to learn how to temper it. She didn't want that for the baby, with his cheerful flailing fists and his contented nature and his very human body. He didn't even have any teeth yet.

And would it even work? She had never heard of a baby like her, and she didn't know anyone she could ask. There were others around – they'd pass each other warily at night, recognise the stink of magic off each other, keep their distance – but she didn't really trust them.

But other times, when she had the heft of him pressed against her, beating heart to beating heart, she thought about what it would be like to keep him just like that, forever. Because she was fairly sure that she wasn't going to die. She never seemed to get any older, though as long as she drank enough blood her body seemed to work as it always had – she had periods, and got spots, and her hair grew, and her heart pumped, and sometimes she hardly felt like she was dead at all. It was too tempting to think of keeping him; she was greedy for it now.

One evening the baby's father came into the sitting room, sat on the couch next to her, ran his hand over the warm velvet of the baby's head. He still had a spatula in his hand, and a tea towel over his shoulder, and he was smiling.

'I've been thinking,' he said, 'that we should try for another one. I've always wanted two.'

53

That night, when the baby woke for the third time, she took him out of the bedroom, and fed him in the sitting room, in the cool gauzy light of predawn. What would it be like, she wondered again, to have the baby plump and needy and devoted forever, her arms an endless cradle? He purred up at her, milk-fat and content, grabbed at a hank of her hair. When she eased his hand open to release it, kissed the swell of his palm below the lifeline, the creases there had a dense, animal smell to them.

Under the thin skin of his scalp, his soft spot pulsed against her questing fingers.

Tim,
the Lantern Holder

Sandy Parsons

Tim picked up the lantern. It was windy on this section of the boardwalk, where the river bowed to accommodate the sea, and a gale must have knocked the lantern from its post. Tim meant to return the object to its duty. But first he held it out with one arm stiff and undulated the rest of his body. His friends, already drunk, laughed. Tim's girlfriend didn't laugh but she raised her cup. He was embarrassed, but the moment had a magical quality, as if he'd been granted some unique status. Passersby pointed and waved. When he put the lantern down to rejoin his friends, they cajoled him. 'Bet you can't do it for an hour.'

Tim could, and did, although he had to keep changing the lantern-holding arm. 'All night?' his rival asked, arm looped like a hook around Tim's girlfriend's neck. When the sun swallowed the lantern's light, Tim felt as if he'd accomplished something. He was trying to figure out how to affix the lantern to the post, which he hadn't noticed was broken. A woman came over and asked if he'd stay for a few minutes; she wanted her son to see that dance. For the children, of course. All day he held the lantern on this corner of the boardwalk, leaving only when hunger overcame him. The next day the clouds rested on the water. Tim returned, with tools, to try and put the lantern back on the post. He didn't tell his friends. How could he explain worrying about an inanimate object's duty? A worker recognized Tim and waved. He held up the lantern, waving like a mock sentinel. A boat passing in the fog bellowed and although it seemed more a joke than a necessity Tim swung the lantern aloft. He hoped his girlfriend would come back and see him, admire his devotion to the task. She did not.

He learned when to switch arms, and when to hold still. The first time Tim stayed all night on the boardwalk he fell asleep on his feet. A pigeon alighting onto the nest of his hair awakened him. The mayor came with an entourage. 'Keep up the good work,' he said, and patted Tim's arm, marveled at the solidity of Tim's lantern-holding bicep. 'Can you perform Tuesday for the parade?' Tim had wanted to visit his mother, had actually been thinking of going and not coming back. 'Okay,' he said, and the smiling faces reassured him he had made the right choice.

Tim practiced holding still for hours at a time. The tactic paid off, better than the dance. He wanted to wave to the people on the floats, wink and dance, but standing still garnered more adulation.

His mother came to visit, after Tim's parade fame reached her. She pressed her palms together when he said he was done, ready to move on to something else. She castigated him with mother logic. 'The little ones love you, and this corner of the boardwalk is so much brighter with you on it.'

Seagulls shat on him, doves preened on his arm, burrowers roamed the paths of his sinews and veins. A child punched him in the stomach and drunken lovers tried to carve their initials into his chest. He became attuned to motion, like a prey animal, yet became inured to vagaries of wind, salt, and rain.

A brushing caress startled Tim to awareness. 'Park maintenance,' said the man, who introduced himself as Vince. 'The mayor wants to make sure your needs are taken care of. So. What do you need...?'

Vince from Park Maintenance had not filled in the words to make the question. Tim realized it was a way of asking his name. But pulling it out was like stretching taffy, and then he had to force the sound through cracked lips. 'Tim.' He needed many things, but he wasn't sure what to ask for first. In the subsequent silence Vince pulled twigs from Tim's hair and pruned the edges of his beard. Vince came by before the sun topped the trees. He had a small broom with which he dusted Tim. He rubbed oil on Tim's burnt skin and checked the lantern's fuel. Sometimes he asked questions that Tim couldn't answer but didn't seem to mind the lack of answers. When he kissed Tim he said, 'Your lips are cold.'

'But my heart is gold.'

Vince laughed, but after a moment he stared at the river wistfully. 'You light up the river, but what do you see of the sea beyond?'

'I like what I see right now,' said Tim, but only because he had forgotten what the other sea meant.

Vince visited often, and talked of his dreams, of what he'd find elsewhere, reminding Tim that he'd had dreams. One day, Vince said, 'We could leave together. If we jump into the river we could ride the current all the way to a new life.'

Tim jumped first, and Vince followed. The current was strong. Tim's legs were like stone, pulling him under, but his arms were strong and he swam up. 'Help,' said Vince, his voice full of water. He was too far away, so Tim climbed on the boardwalk and shone his light for the rescuers. For three days they searched, but if Vince's body was ever found, nobody told Tim.

Tim's feet became stuck to the boardwalk, encrusted by barnacles and salt from the sea. People covered him with blankets in the cold and when they remembered, left nuts and bread. Once a kindly stranger held their coat over him during a rainstorm, until their companion laughed and drew them away.

One windy day the mayor visited, attended by workers with buckets and brushes. 'We made a resin to keep you warm. Better than the blankets.' Tim remembered that clothes were better than blankets. He admired the way the mayor had sway over the others. He nodded and they scraped away the barnacles before painting him, and the lantern, too. The scraping hurt, but not much. The mayor was right about the resin. Once it hardened he was more comfortable.

Someone was brushing him. He remembered loving hands, being touched like a human. But this was Park Maintenance, a young girl, unfamiliar in dress and speech. She spoke to him as she polished, and asked questions, but Tim's mouth no longer had the power of speech.

A Man
Is Fishing on
the Bank of a River

Samuel Skuse

He is not an especially old man, but old enough to notice
that the bank has gradually eroded over the years he has
stood upon it. His arms are strong and a greying beard hides
his mouth. He comes here once or twice each summer, except
for the year of his divorce when he spent most of the warm
evenings drinking beer, and watching the dragonflies glis-
ten in the fading light. Back then he would stand for hours,
his rod attached to his hand like an extension of himself.
He would catch fish back then too. Tench, perch, eels, even
trout; he would come home with a collection that a fishmon-
ger would be proud of. Now his aching knees have resigned
him to his folding chair, and he can barely remember the
last time he caught anything other than leaves in dark, tarry
clogs. But in truth, with the passing years, the thought of
catching a fish and watching it struggle for breath or bashing
it against a rock until it stops wriggling has seemed more and
more barbaric and sad. So, though he continues to fish, he
does so with very little real conviction. The fish themselves,

always visible in the glassy waters, are more than obliging in showing little to no interest in the man's bait. Sometimes, after fruitless fishing trips, he stops by the market on the way home to buy fresh fish. He has a suspicion as to why he does this, but would never admit it to anyone.

There is no one reason why the man returns to this spot year after year, but many. He likes the way the light skips off the river's surface like a stone. He likes the way the trees at his back whisper words in their own language. He likes the way the insects dart around in the air like a busy intersection. He likes the way the loneliness feels here. It's a loneliness that is absolute and self-imposed and euphoric. But most of all, he just likes that this place is always *here*. The banks may shorten as the years trickle by, but when they are gone, he may sit in the branches of the trees. And if the trees are felled by a storm, he may use the wood to build a boat to sit upon the water. Or he may float high above and look down on this place as a cloud melting into a painted sky.

A man is fishing on the bank of a river. One of these days he imagines that he will wade into these waters and allow the gentle current to carry him away to whatever may be waiting for him downstream. A dragonfly's wings hum softly in the man's ears as he drinks in the last of the dwindling light. Stillness settles like a veil.

Where the Sun Is Always Setting

Daniel Ray

Luis put a log on the fire and watched it burn.

Out in the dark, past the reach of the firelight, something made a noise. Luis knew better than to look. He checked his watch, almost midnight. There was no wind. His fire was burning steady and time was passing slowly. He took another log from the lumber pile and dropped it on the fire and waited. There wasn't anything else to do.

Luis was almost halfway through his shift: ten to six – the night shift. Only the best Burners were allowed to work at night, and if Luis wasn't the best, he was certainly the most experienced; he had been keeping the fires burning for almost seven years. The Burners who came before him were gone. All of them. Burners last a long time or they don't last long at all. Luis had lasted. His secret was simple: don't look into the darkness. Only it wasn't a secret. Every Burner knew not to look. Some did anyway, and once they did, they were done. Luis had seen it happen before. They get up and walk away from the fire and they're gone. It had never happened to one of Luis' partners, only his neighbours.

61

Luis looked to the west. Eighty yards away another fire was burning in the dark. Two men were standing by the fire, one watching the flames, the other watching him. Luis looked to the east. Two men, another fire, one watching the fire, one watching him.

He signalled to the men that everything was okay, then went back to watching his fire. A few hours after midnight an old man pushing a wheelbarrow full of split wood walked into the firelight.

'That you, Jackson?' Luis asked.

'Don't know who else it'd be,' Jackson answered.

Jackson was usually smiling, and at night you could see his teeth before you saw the rest of him. Jackson was always on time, always upbeat, and most importantly, he always brought plenty of firewood. Luis wasn't sure why, but there was someone walking behind Jackson, a boy he didn't recognize.

Jackson said, 'You stayin' busy, Luis?'

That's what Jackson always said.

And Luis always replied, 'Not as busy as you, old man.'

Jackson laughed and parked the wheelbarrow beside the fire and said, 'Brought you a brand new Burner. Luis, this is Elijah. Elijah, Luis.'

The young man stepped forward and stuck out his hand and Luis shook it. Luis started to tell Jackson that he had forgotten it was Monday – starting day for new Burners – but he stopped himself. Luis didn't want anyone to think he was slipping and lose confidence. He was proud to be the only perimeter guard who was allowed to work alone, and enjoyed guiding new Burners through their first shift.

Luis let go of the boy's hand and said, 'How old are you, kid?'

'Eighteen.'

Luis looked at Jackson and Jackson shrugged.

Twenty had always been the minimum age for Burners, but the town council had been tinkering with the idea of lowering the minimum age to eighteen. Luis knew there was no use getting upset about it; he was well respected among his fellow Fire-Burners, but his opinion didn't carry any weight with the council.

Luis stepped back and took a good look at Elijah.

'Glad to have you, no matter how old you are,' Luis said. 'Go ahead and check your kit.'

'Yes, sir,' Elijah said, and slung a small backpack off his shoulder.

Every Burner was issued a fire kit – a backpack filled with things they might need: matches, lighters, flares, strike strips. But the most important thing in the kit was a glass jar filled with gasoline. The boy unpacked his bag and took inventory. It was all there.

After Elijah repacked his kit, the three of them made small talk as they unloaded wood from the wheelbarrow. Jackson let the younger men do most of the work. Luis didn't mind. He wasn't sure how old Jackson was, but guessed him to be somewhere between sixty and seventy, maybe older.

'You about done for the night?' Luis asked.

'No, but I'll get there,' Jackson answered. He stretched his back before grabbing the wheelbarrow handles. 'See you again tomorrow night. Keep your eyes down, new kid.'

Jackson disappeared into the darkness. Luis jostled the coals then put a fresh log on the fire. He looked at Elijah. His eyes were white around the edges, his face expressionless. He was scared.

'You can look if you want to,' Luis said.

'I thought we weren't supposed to look.'

'We're not, but if you can't handle one look then you have no business being out here.'

Elijah's eyes grew wider. He shifted on his feet, his body rigid. He turned and looked into the darkness and Luis thought he could see figures reflecting in the boy's eyes, but maybe it was just his imagination.

'That's enough,' Luis said, and Elijah's gaze turned back to the fire. 'What did you see?'

'Something moving in the trees. Is that them?

'Yes.'

'Are they always there?'

'Always.'

It was true. They never left, never gave the Burners a single moment of rest. Seven years had passed since they came, but it felt like a lifetime. A life spent in a state of constant vigilance was torture, and the endless nights were beginning to affect Luis in ways he couldn't understand. He had no desire to spend the rest of his life staring into the fire, but he had no other choice.

'Do you know the signals?' Luis asked.

'Yes, sir. I learned them all – I think.'

'Good, then you can say hello to our neighbours.'

Elijah looked east then west and said, 'Why are they watching me?'

'Probably because there's nothing else to do. Go ahead and wave.'

Elijah waved. Luis watched the little movements of Elijah's face – the involuntary spasms of someone performing sign language. None of the Burners knew real sign language, but they developed their own system for communication: basic gestures made with arms instead of hands. You can't see someone's hands very well at eighty yards, especially at night.

Elijah suddenly looked worried.

'What does this sign mean?' he asked.

Elijah touched the tips of his fingers together and stuck his elbows out and moved his arms up and down slowly.

'It means calm down,' Luis said, laughing softly. 'I know it's your first night on the perimeter, but you gotta take it easy. There's nothing difficult about this job, unless a storm blows in.'

Elijah quickly made the goodbye gesture to the east and west then said, 'What's it like? A storm I mean. I've heard things.'

Luis wanted to say, '*It's worse than you can imagine,*' but he held his tongue. He didn't want to scare the kid on his first shift.

Luis would never forget his first storm. It had lasted all night. Eight hours of hard work tending the fire, eight hours of fear and adrenaline. Luis had been plagued with night-mares for months after the storm had passed. The dreams always ended the same way: with the fires going out. He would wake up in a panic, still trying to feed the fire, feeding the blankets off his bed into the floor. Over the years Luis had learned that his fellow Burners suffered from similar night-mares; besides always smelling like smoke, it was one of the few things they all had in common.

To keep from scaring the kid, Luis said, 'Storms aren't so bad. You stay busy until they're over. That's about it.'

It wasn't a whole lie.

'So, what happens if the fire does go out?' Elijah asked.

'You use your gasoline.'

'What if that doesn't work? What if the fire goes all the way out?'

'It's our job to keep that from happening, no matter what.'

They stood staring at the flames for a while. There was nowhere to sit, no chair to get comfortable in, nowhere to fall asleep.

'You ever had a fire almost go out?'

The boy couldn't let it go, but Luis didn't blame him.

'I've had one go all the way out,' Luis answered.

'What did you do?'

'I got it going again.'

'Was it during a storm?'

'Actually, no. It was a good night and the sky was clear. Then out of nowhere a gust of wind put out my neighbours fire. He was alone. His partner had... retired earlier that same night. He panicked and dropped his gasoline, so I did the only thing I could do: I grabbed my jar and took a log from my fire and took off in a dead run.' Luis held out his left hand and let the boy look at it. The skin was smooth and shiny and pink. 'I didn't have time to put on gloves, but I hardly felt it.'

Luis gestured and Elijah put a log on the fire.

'You got the fire going again in time?' the boy asked.

'Barely. They came out of the trees. I could see them coming, hundreds of them. When I got the fire lit I could see their eyes. Probably could've reached out and touched one of them if I wanted.'

Luis still had nightmares about it.

Sometimes he didn't get the fire going in time.

Sometimes he woke up screaming.

'Why do you think they're here?' Elijah asked under his breath, like he wasn't allowed to talk about them.

Luis said, 'I don't know.'

'My mother used to say it's because Hell got full. She said there wasn't anywhere else for them to go.'

'I've heard people say that.'

'Have you ever...' Elijah paused.

'Ever what?'

Elijah leaned in.

'You ever seen someone you know standing out there?'

'No, and I hope I never do.'

Truth was, Luis had never looked long enough to recognize any of them.

'They told me you've been out here longer than anyone,' Elijah said.

'It's true.'

'Is that why they let you work alone?'

'I guess.'

Luis crouched down and crossed his arms and rested his elbows on his knees and stared into the fire. He could still remember what the world had been like before, and he often thought about those last few days before everything changed.

He thought it was some kind of prank at first. You're looking at your phone and you see a story about a dozen people who died of carbon monoxide poisoning waking up on their way to the morgue, you think it's clickbait. You see a video about a kid who came back to life after spending six hours underwater, you wonder if anyone really believes that crap.

But it was true.

One day in late November, the dead started coming back to life worldwide. Cancer, suicide, old age – no matter the cause, they all came back. At first, they were catatonic. They would hardly speak. They wouldn't eat or drink. Some people called them zombies though they did not eat flesh, and some called them vampires though they did not drink blood. The dead looked the same as the living, until you got close enough to see their eyes, empty and lifeless, dead and gone.

It wasn't long before the dead became violent. People found out the hard way that they'll hold you down and choke the life out of you, first chance they get. Killers, all of them. Why, no one knows.

The dead begat the dead, and it wasn't long until the dead outnumbered the living.

It happened very quickly.

Luis had left the city driving west and stumbled across Harpers Landing by chance. The fires were already burning. A woman named Sandra Beckett had been the one to discover that fire repelled the dead, and the fires had been burning day and night ever since. Sandra was gone. Most of the original survivors were gone.

Luis stood up and looked to his neighbours. The fires were still burning. The night was quiet and the winds were calm.

He said, 'Nights like these are easy, but you always have to watch out for your neighbours. Anything could happen.'

'Like what?' Elijah asked.

'Someone could fall asleep or have a heart attack or anything.' Luis didn't want to say what he was thinking but he had to. 'And someone could abandon their post.'

'You mean, *retire?*'

'Yes.'

'How often does it happen?'

'It's pretty rare.'

'But you've seen people just… leave?'

'I have,' Luis said, and checked his watch. 'You hungry?'

'I don't know.'

Luis took his lunch out of his pack (homemade bread and steamed potatoes) and began eating. Not long after the dead had returned, the people of Harper's Landing realised how important it was going to be to have crops, so every couple months they had pushed the fire perimeter out a little farther into the fields that surrounded the town until they finally reached the woods. Harpers Landing was an old farming community, so they had enough equipment to tend the fields. The town itself was just one long street – old brick buildings mostly. The town sat in a natural bowl at the edge of a river (the fish had been harvested to extinction within the first year) and was surrounded by low, rolling hills. It was the perfect place to live, maybe the only place left to live.

'Why do you think the fires keep them back?' the boy asked.

'I don't know,' Luis said. 'Maybe it's like your mother said. Maybe all those dead people know they're supposed to be in Hell. Maybe that's why they're afraid of flames.'

Luis meant it to come across as a joke but Elijah didn't take it that way. What little colour was left in the boy's face drained away.

'Hey, I was kidding. You gotta lighten up.'

Out in the darkness, something made a noise.

'What was that?' Elijah said, his voice high and bright.

Luis doubted Elijah would make it a week, and he wasn't sure how the kid got approved to be a Burner in the first place. That wasn't true. Deep down, Luis knew why: there wasn't anyone else. The town's population was dwindling. Years had passed since a new survivor had arrived. There wasn't enough food and medicine to repopulate; most newborn babies didn't live very long. And going out to scavenge for supplies and cut trees for the fires was getting more and more dangerous.

The scavenger crews carried fire with them on a table-like contraption. They had to move slowly but it kept the dead back. It had always made Luis think of the Hebrews carrying the Ark of the Covenant, four men holding fire on two long poles. It seemed appropriate – the fires were sacred, more important than anything else. But the scavenger crews often came back with one less person than they left with. And lately, Burners had been retiring at an alarming rate.

Time was running out.

The sun was setting on Harpers Landing, and there wasn't anything anyone could do to stop it.

Looking at Elijah, Luis could see exactly what he had looked like as a child.

The boy was shaking.

'How'd you come to be here, Elijah?' Luis asked.

He needed to bring the boy back, ground him before he got any worse.

'What? Uh, me and my mother came together, about five years ago.'

'I think I remember that. You were driving a red van, right?'

'Yeah, it belonged to our neighbours. We figured they didn't need it anymore. We ran out of food at home so we had to leave.'

Luis did the math.

'You and your mother made it two years by yourself at home?'

'Yeah, my dad was kind of a prepper, so we had a basement full of food. He was at work the day the dead started coming back. He never came home. It was just the two of us, me and mom. We made the food last.' There was a silence. 'How about you?'

Luis said, 'I've been here since the end, or the beginning – however you want to look at it. Seven years, how time flies.'

'Time passes differently here, doesn't it?'

'It does.'

Elijah seemed to be calming down; he took a hunk of bread from his pack and began nibbling on it. As he ate, he spoke:

'When we first got here, I couldn't sleep, so I used to stay up at night and watch the fires. I always thought it looked like a sunset, all the fires burning on the horizon, like a sunset at night.' He shoved the last of the bread in his mouth and chewed. 'Sometimes I would hear my mother crying. She missed my dad. I did too, but I think she did more. I don't think she ever got used to living here.' He stared at the fire for a long time. 'I miss her.'

Luis said, 'What happened?'

'Frankie said it was cancer.'

Frankie Watts was a nurse practitioner, and the closest thing Harpers Landing had to a doctor. She was good. She had saved a lot of people's lives. But she couldn't save everybody.

'Sorry to hear that,' Luis said.

'Have you lost anyone?' Elijah asked.

'Not since it started. I came here alone.'

Luis thought of his grandma. She had raised him, was a mother to him. He had watched her die. The dead broke into their house and killed her. There was nothing he could do to save her, and he couldn't bear to watch her come back, so he ran. It was getting harder to remember her face, but if he saw her out in the dark watching him, he was certain he would recognise her.

Elijah said, 'Before my mom died they gave her two options. You know what they were?'

Luis knew, but Elijah wasn't really asking.

'"We can burn you on a pyre, or you can leave."' Can you believe that? Those were the choices they gave her. Burn or walk into the woods. What a choice.' Elijah laughed and shook his head. He stared into the flames, his eyes glowing orange. 'My mother refused to be burnt. She didn't think it was right. So they pulled her up here to the perimeter in a cart and told her to walk. She hadn't walked in weeks, but somehow she did. They were nice enough to let me come and say goodbye. Then she walked out into the woods by herself, and I just stood there.' He began to sniffle, his voice cracking. 'I still can't believe she made it, but she did.' Tears pouring down his face, he looked out into the darkness and said, 'I'd really like to see her again.'

Luis clapped his hands and shouted, 'Hey!' Elijah turned to face Luis. 'Don't look out there. You won't see anything good. I understand that you want to see your mother again, but she's gone.'

Elijah turned back to the trees.

'I can see them. I can see their eyes shining. It's the fire. I can see the fire in their eyes.'

'Elijah!'

Luis raced to the other side of the fire and grabbed the boy and looked into his eyes and saw everything that was going to happen in the coming months: the food getting low, people getting scared, then angry, the town council members being lynched in the streets. Even if that didn't happen, Harpers Landing wouldn't last another year. Luis knew it like he knew the sun would rise. If they were sending kids like Elijah to keep the fires, they were getting to the bottom of the barrel, and sooner or later, someone would let the fires go out.

Luis let Elijah go and the boy fell to the ground.

'Let me tell you something most people don't know,' Luis said, the boy looking up at him. 'Our loved ones want us. They seek us out. So yes, your mother is probably out there. My grandma might be too. That's why Burners abandon their stations. They get lonely. They see their wife or their husband or their kids out there in the dark and they can't help but go to them. But it's not them. You have to know that. It's not them. They're gone.'

Luis went back to his side of the fire, and Elijah stood up and wiped his face on his shirt. Luis wouldn't look at him.

They didn't talk much the rest of the night, and six a.m. came slowly. Two new Burners came and took Luis and Elijah's place – two women. It was only a ten minute walk back to town, all slightly downhill. Elijah went one way and Luis went the other. Luis had a room at the old motel on Main Street; being a longtime resident had its perks. Luis assumed that Elijah lived in the bunkhouse (an old firehouse) with the other Burners.

The night had been uneventful for the most part, but Luis felt completely drained. Part of him was glad that it was almost over. Not just the night, but everything. Luis had accepted the truth: nothing lasts forever. He wondered if it would be better to just go ahead and put the fires out and get it over with.

He climbed a set of stairs to the second floor of the motel and walked along the balcony to his room. He unlocked the door and went inside and dropped his bag and dug around in his nightstand until he found a pack of cigarettes and a lighter. He went back outside, leaned against the railing, and looked at the horizon. Sunrise wasn't for another half hour, but it wasn't dark, not all the way. It was never really dark in Harpers Landing.

Luis shook the last cigarette out of the pack and held it between his fingers, maybe the last cigarette on Earth. He had been saving it for a long time. No matter what happened, he could always have a cigarette if he wanted. Just knowing that kept him going some nights.

Luis stuck the cigarette in his mouth and lit it and took a long drag. He coughed. It didn't taste right. The tobacco had gone bad. He wasn't surprised, or even disappointed. Everything had an expiration date, and there was no reason to get upset about it.

His thoughts wandered to his grandma. Luis missed her so much it hurt, and he wanted to see her again more than anything. He tried to take another drag from the cigarette, but the smoke tasted terrible, like wood smoke. He flicked the cigarette over the railing and took one last look at the horizon before going inside.

The sunset and the sunrise were merging and the sky was turning the richest shade of orange that Luis had ever seen.

He had never realized how beautiful it truly was.

Disloyal Order

Courtney Smyth

I would follow Emma anywhere, and that is why I am in this club.

This club, with its pulsing trap beats and bad vodka and too many people I don't know, all piled in on top of each other pretending to have a good time. Bodies pressed against bodies, sweat condensing on the ceiling, and me in the middle of it all, not sure I should be.

But she is here with me – or rather, I am here with her. The order of who brings who where is Emma-first, always. Emma and Fi, Fi and Emma, inseparable opposites and charming facsimiles. We're here. I try to enjoy it. Doing anything lately has been a dread fest, but once I'm out, once I'm present, I can't hate it.

Especially not when I'm with her.

It's not new for me to be led random places by Emma; I've a history of following her everywhere. In school they'd call me her lapdog, which was as inaccurate then as it was dehumanising, but over the years it really did get easier to just let her pick the place. Pick the bar. The holiday destination. The tattoo studio where we got matching tattoos, aged 18. Whenever I look at it – my only tattoo – I can feel the needle piercing my skin over and over, a permanent reminder of our years so far and our years to come. She volunteered me to go first that time – probably the only time I'd ever gone first in anything we'd done together, and that should've been a hint. Emma got hers covered up inside of a couple of weeks. I'd laughed when I saw the replacement, months later, because it's just like her to do something together, then do the opposite apart.

Anything goes with Emma, and I ride it out. It's never as bad as I think it'll be. I can always talk myself around.

Tonight, I am wearing a dress she insisted I put on and we're dancing to a song with no discernible beginning, middle or end. I make eye contact with her, laughing as she bats away various men wrong enough to think they could get a second of her time. Her time is for me tonight. No one else.

These are the moments that make us worth it. These are the moments that make us good.

'I've missed you!' Emma shouts, and she waves her phone at me, holding it up into the flashing lights and posing, waving me in beside her to take a photo.

Our friendship is literally defined in these snapshots. Moments we can remember when tucked into bed after a takeaway, pulling bits of glitter from our hair, my makeup usually smeared across my face still, and her admonishing me that I will not always be this young, will not always have this face, this body, this life. Reminding me to enjoy it. Telling me she loves me. That I am special. That I am important.

She used to remember to miss me all the time.

We're in the smoking area now. That's most nights with her – bar, dance, toilet, outside, repeat. Break in the routine if someone catches her attention, where I'm left to stand awkwardly to the side nursing a drink. So far she's focused on me. Our breath fogs in front of our faces. She doesn't actually smoke, of course, but there's an unlit cigarette hanging from her lips as she flicks through the camera roll, landing on photos from last summer.

I wish I had a coat. The pressing heat evaporates quickly and dries on my skin, a clinging residue I'll have to endure for the rest of the night.

'Oh my god, Fi, do you remember Knockanstocken?' she asks.

Of course I do. It's one of the last big things we did together before life got in the way.

'Those poor Mayo lads,' I laugh. This is what I'm supposed to say.

We'd piled our stuff into her brother's car and drove up on a whim. I bought the tickets, she provided the car. A fair trade at the time, I felt. We met the two poor lads in question outside the camp grounds. They'd carried our stuff for us and then built our tent – though it was for Emma, really. All of it was for Emma. She bats her eyes and flicks her hair and pretends she doesn't know what's going on and before anyone can think about it they're falling over themselves to help her. Make her feel better. She's someone you want to take care of, like. Even I feel it a bit sometimes.

'It's been so long since we've gotten to do something like that,' I say, because I know that's what I should say next.

'Yeah, well. Your contact hours were ridiculous, and I had placement.' She makes a face and I mimic it.

Everything had changed and it meant an end to getting ready to go out together, or me dropping round to hers to drink badly made gin martinis while we watched old episodes of cookery shows or movies starring actors that were something, once. She used to say we'd never be like that. That we'd never fade; we'd burn brighter than anything.

That weekend away had been everything.

'I miss that.' I say. 'I miss us.'

She pouts instead of saying anything, but I know she misses it too; once a month she posts one of her countless photos of her posing with drinks, or showing off the thrifted outfits she'd pulled together, captioned "take me back" or some variant of it.

'I'm done,' she says, pocketing her cigarette, and she takes my hand for a brief second. Frozen, reddened fingers in mine. Her nails bitten, mine immaculate.

I'm never in the photos, but I know I was there and that's all that matters.

She's dragging me in a different direction. I hadn't realised this club, already too hot, the abrupt return of warmth burning my skin, had another room to it. She screeches something inaudible as we reach it. The music here has words, finally, a mix of cheesy 2000s and pop-rock that makes me feel like summer and hot cars and driving and like nothing could ever be wrong, and I feel myself relaxing. I try to make a beeline for the dance floor, stumbling on the heels Emma insisted I wear because they match the dress. It was always easier to agree.

It takes me an embarrassingly long minute to realise she is running the opposite way, throwing her arms around Dave; familiar face, harbinger of dread.

We dated once, me and Dave, after I accidentally kissed him at her birthday, leading to coolness between Emma and me that spanned weeks but felt like it had lasted decades.

Emma said that it was a bad idea. Me and Dave. After the event.

'You used to know where your loyalties lie,' she'd said, as if I could've known what would happen. That it would happen. That I shouldn't have done it, that it would do this to us.

I cried for hours in therapy over Dave and at her insistence on keeping Dave as her friend only and my therapist had asked, *was she worth it?*

She was.

She had been.

She is.

I could sometimes endure Dave for her. It's easier this way.

Friendships are always measured in years, decades, spans of time, and Emma had been my friend since the very first day of secondary school, sitting next to each other in every class, where she deftly wound up every teacher then sat back to let the chaos unfold around her. She never meant to be chaotic, I don't think. This is just how she is wired. Chaos follows her everywhere, and I only recently noticed. Sometimes it's hard to keep up.

Dave whispered something in her ear and Emma shoots a glance back at me. It could be guilt. I pretend it is.

I mime going to the bar because I don't want to see Dave, I don't want to know Dave. His presence is ruining what this night is meant to be. It's not jealousy; it's wariness. Sadness he is still in my life. Weariness. Words I have typed over and over again in texts to Emma, trying to make her understand how much I didn't want to ever be in the same room as him again, much less the same club, hearing the same songs and breathing the same, stale air.

I order, eventually, a space carved out at the bar, my stomach pressed against the sticky wood, wondering how many hands and how many drinks have rested there before me. How many moments and friendships are imprinted in the ghosts of nights out gone by, how long this wooden bar has stood and how many people have lost their thoughts in it.

Three Jaegerbombs for a tenner. I down two. Hold the third one for Emma, cupped between my two hands, fizzing, nebulous, cloying. She is still sort of wrapped around Dave, he is still awful, looking over her shoulder at me with a smile on his face that I do not like and I still don't want to see him.

'It's just easier to stay on speaking terms with him.'

That's what her responding text had read, when I finally got the words out. When I could finally explain to her what the problem was. When she had finally replied, days later.

I drink the third.

I stack the empty cups on the bar and slip away from it. I don't want anything else. I have work in the morning. I want to go home.

The song changed then, familiar bars forcing a reaction out of me, my face breaking into the first real smile of the night.

Our song.

She'd write the words inside cards, when she remembered cards, on birthdays and at Christmas. I'd had a t-shirt with lyrics from it printed for her, one time. I don't think she ever wore it, but that was never the point. The point is always the reminder of something that is primarily *us*.

She turns as the verse starts, meets my gaze, runs across the dancefloor. It is hazy now. Dry ice and sticky-sweet liquor coats my tongue as she grabs my hands and twirls me. I am still spinning when I turn to face her, everything right again – bar the dark cloud in the corner. He is still here and I am being squeezed out of this room, inch by inch, drop by drop, wrung tightly by his gaze.

When the chorus hits, she lets go of my hands and whirls away. I barely register that she's gone. I am packed in tightly by bodies, though I might as well be alone, arms limp by my sides as I resign myself to moving towards her, sheepish and slow on borrowed heels.

'This is my best friend Aoife,' Emma says.

She does not say *this is my best friend, Aoife*.

There is no pause.

'Aoife, this is Fi.'

The names are in the wrong order. There is no comma, no beat. She looks at me as she makes the introduction, as though it has not just caused sickening terror to work its way down into my stomach, following the burning path of the Jaeger, and settling there dreadfully as though it would never leave.

I am Fi, this girl is Aoife.

I am not so naïve, so childlike, to believe that Best Friend is a single crown granted to a single wearer, but Aoife holds her hands and they are dancing to our song and Dave is still in the corner and I remember, suddenly, the nights she did not reply to my messages or the day I sobbed in the corner of the college library over my parents finally divorcing, my desperate calls to Emma unanswered, the Instagram stories she'd posted moments later of her sitting in her house with five friends I'd never heard of, the sounds of my texts buzzing through to her phone audible over her laughing.

Maybe that was the first day of her being this Emma, and this Emma is a stranger. I look at her, my eyes seeing her for the first time. Seeing her face and her cold hands and her body and the unfamiliar way she holds herself, her hair and her makeup and her clothes, things I would've sworn a few minutes ago I knew everything about, could've described perfectly. The person I thought I'd bring to my future wedding, would travel the world with me. Would be my ride-or-die, forever, no question, always there.

I don't know her. I don't know her at all. I've never known her.

When the chorus hits again, Emma and Aoife jump up and down and Emma does not spare me a glance and this feels stupid, for both of us. It feels stupid to be twenty-three and pretending we are the same people we were at thirteen, one the portent of chaos, and the other so willing to be led anywhere in exchange for loyalty.

Dave is still in the corner. He sees my face. He knows me, and I hate this. He knows me even though we did not date for long, not with the way Emma was about the whole thing, not with the way she said that a breakup would ruin her college friend group, that they would stop choosing her because of me, that every bad, sad thing that could happen, would happen to her. How was that fair?

I agreed at the time. It was easiest to agree.

Dave's gaze meets mine, an anchor in the room that brings me back to my body.

Dave knows.

Was she worth it?

I wanted so badly to believe that the therapist was lying, but I can hear her now, speaking right into my ear as though she is standing limp-armed and defeated beside me, with me. I want to go back in time to that room and tell her not to talk about my friend like that, my best friend, and maybe this wouldn't be happening now.

Emma and Fi, Fi and Emma, inseparable opposites and charming facsimiles.

My eyes are cloudy, not with drinks or dry ice or even Dave – though he is looking at me with such pity I want to scream – but with tears as the chorus hits again and she doesn't look at me and I know, now, what I had known on that first day of school when she'd left me to sit alone at lunch. What I'd known in the tattoo shop chair when she made a face at how the tattoo she'd picked looked on me. What I'd known the day in the festival tent when she had taken the two Mayo boys off and left me a shivering, puking mess because I had eaten something bad from a food truck.

I've just never believed any of it before.

My body starts to pull me away. Away from the scene. Away from the bodies. From Dave. From Emma. From the chaos.

Emma hasn't noticed. She and Aoife move to the bar.

I leave without my coat.

# of wood and stone, and gilded bones

Mei Davis

*Tell no one your name. Tell none where you have
come from. Embed yourself into the Daimyo's
household, and never look his samurai in the eyes, for
a true warrior always recognises one of its own.*

It is summer in Mikawa Province, the sixteenth year of
Tenbun, a time of monsoons and warring.

Morning embarks across the sky, and with it the sun,
the heat, the chorus of shrieking cicadas in tow. You groan.
Stretch. Push yourself up from a rancid tatami mat as you do
every morning, drenched in sweat and a throbbing resentment.

Stop. Remember your training. Discard your feelings,
along with the night. Don your daylight disguise: sloppy
grins and a peal of yawning laughter.

'What a beautiful sunrise!' you say to the dishevelled
throng. The other outcasts stir, awake into another dawn of

misery. Like you, they live as exiles along the outskirts of the village. Like you, they sleep as livestock beneath the boiling skies. Unlike you, they do it all for free. 'Did we really survive another night?'

Children clothed in filth point and laugh. For a moment, they've forgotten their bloated bellies. The old and withered pause in moaning over their bedsores.

Only Yoshio frowns at your antics, and wags a limp finger. It is all he is able to lift, his arms the texture of *umeboshi*, shrivelled salt plums sagging off his needle-thin bones. 'Only the rich can afford to make jokes out of life and death. So which are you, Hideo?'

Ignore the way his shrewd eyes unmask you, the way he smells of rot. Instead, divert his suspicion with simple sleight of hand. See the grey stone? Smooth as a coin. Now it is gone. Here again, behind Taka's ear.

Laughter and applause.

Time to work. Wave farewell. Sweep inwards towards the village proper. Pass through the merchant quarters, farmers bent over flooded rice paddies, sturdy craftsmen shops where carpenters hunch over great blocks of cedar and elm. Along the way ask, 'Any rubbish?' It is your job to carry away their garbage and refuse, and you are the only one who does it with such fervour, a hop and grin all the way to the steaming dumps.

You reach the village by noon. The cicadas have quieted, replaced by the incessant barks of the marketplace. Kashigawa castle looms over the flat-roofed stalls like a mantis over its prey. A fitting analogy. Don't they feast upon them with their taxes and protection schemes? The nobility, the samurai, the fat purses of the daimyos – the blood of the poor nourishing the veins of the rich.

Don't dwell on grievances. The castle, remember, is a mass producer of waste, your biggest client. They give you more than you can carry in one trip. It takes two. Three. Thirteen. They pay you in grains of rice, and you are thankful. 'Come back tomorrow, Hideo!' No one knows your name. None know where you have come from. But Hideo is an icon in this haemorrhaging village. 'Was it not Hideo who helped Satori-san pick his crop when his sons fell ill? Saved the whole family from being sold off when the tax collectors came round.'

You are everyone's favourite outcast.

At dusk, footsore and dehydrated, you lean against the castle walls. They are a puzzle of boulders and stones pieced together and stacked an imposing twenty feet high, the white and grey castle perched atop like a flock of birds, its arched rooftops a flurry of wings. You have never once stepped foot inside, and kick at the stony base.

A face pops out of a first floor window.

'Hideo?' Daizou, one of the domestic foremen. 'Is that you under all that dirt?'

Simper and laugh, make the fool feel clever. '*Hai, hai!*'

'I'm glad I caught you.' He tosses out a half-eaten apple. You catch it, smell it, rip into its browning flesh, juice dribbling down your chin. 'Kando-san tells me you were a great help during last week's flooding,' Daizou calls down. 'Saved his whole crop.'

'Nothing, Daizou-san, nothing at all.' Bow three times. These middle manager types love a good honouring. 'Nothing but your humble servant.'

Daizou taps his nose. 'I see what you're about. Still after a proper job, aren't you?'

'Nothing but your good will, Daizou-san.' Bow three times more.

'You'll be happy to hear that I've talked it over with the boss. We need more hands in the house, but it won't be good work – chamber pots and scraps for the compost.' He shivers.

87

A cadre of samurai advance out of the gaping mouth of the wall, armour banging and rumbling, thunder marching on parade. This time, you bow so low your nose touches the ground, and not one of them pays you a glance.

Only their dust clouds remain. 'It would be an honour, Daizou-san,' you say to the dirt.

The castle doors open, and you walk inside.

Locate the inner keep. Find the target. Gain access to both, but do not rouse suspicion. And do not enter the presence of the Daimyo, for an owner of men can sense the will of one he has not purchased.

Within the castle, everything thrives. Faces are full and placid. Painted silk glides over cedar walls, over cushions and pale skin. Light and sound are filtered through a barrier of shoji screens which transform the air into a creamy gauze, as if living in a bottle of milk.

Most unnerving is the sea of winking gold – layers of gilt on everything from furniture to jewellery to ornate mould-ing. How do they not go blind from its glow? Perhaps that is why they miss the way your slippers make no sound on the tatami mats. Or how clumsy Hideo can melt out of a crowd in a blink, materialize out of shadows and corners as an un-earthly *yokai*. There, not there – perhaps always there, like a raindrop in a well, or a poor servant in a rich man's home.

One morning you tap Daizou on the shoulder and he leaps as though he's been struck with a knife. 'Hideo!' One hand grips his heaving chest. The other retracts quickly from within the deep folds of his kimono, the splashes and songs of women bathing in the courtyard below drifting in from the open window. 'I thought I was alone. How long have you been here?' The censure in his voice does nothing to dilute the guilt.

'All along, all along.' Clang your empty chamber pots together to ease the voyeur's shame. 'They eat so much in here the next load is sure to come soon, and always we must be ready for the drop!' Sheepish laugh. 'But could you tell me where these go? Every room looks just the same as the one that came before.'

'These rooms are private. Not for the likes of you.' He wags a finger. Don't stare at his hand, plump and festooned with rings. Don't think of Yoshio and his scolds, the skeleton glued to his mat who will be dead before you ever leave this place. 'I like your work ethic,' he says, 'but you shouldn't go wandering around. There are rules here. Restrictions.'

Bow your head. 'It won't happen again.'

Day is an illusion. You empty the chamber pots, clean them till your eager smile is reflected in the copper. Tell quaint jokes and kowtow at every bread crumb brushed to your side of the floor. Wage a gentle war, a war of slow attrition. Peel off their caution, skin them of their doubts – second by second, inch by inch, until their trust in you is implicit.

'Hideo, I have good news. Takeshi's fallen ill. One of the carnal ailments.' Daizou gestures to his groin and pulls a face. 'What an embarrassment to the household! But it means you've been promoted. You'll be tasked with clearing out the waste in the inner keep – that's where the Daimyo and his family sleep.'

'And the Daimyo's hostages?'

His eyes become slits. 'No one tends to their rooms but me.'

Day is an illusion, and when dusk surrenders to darkness you release the facades to reveal guile and speed. You robe yourself in sable silence and bleed into the night, ink against a black canvas – invisible. Steal away to the unfamiliar, forbidden parts of the castle. Form a map in your mind. Right turns. Left turns. Number of paces and the clockwork rotation of guards. Highlight the passageways triggered with creaky floorboards, the blind corners where a sword can easily wait in hiding for an outstretched neck.

Only once you see the Daimyo, and only his left shoulder, as a shoji screen is cracked to allow in a bit of air. Heavy rainfall batters the shingled roofs as you hang upside down from the eaves, peering at his fine silk kimono, a restive throwing blade twitching in your palm.

How easy.

Stop. Remember your mission. You were sent here for another purpose. 'You will know her,' they told you, 'by her hair, which she leaves unwashed and unpinned, in perpetual mourning for her fate.'

Mourning. What do the rich have to mourn, but a long and easy life?

A lone owl haunts the silence. The moon breaks free of its cloudy prison. Leave no silhouette against the streaming silver light. Conceal the glint of sharp steel as you prowl along the parapets, dancing around the shifting guards to the correct room – fourth floor, two left turns, down the second corridor along the outside wall.

A clear glass wind chime hangs from the sill.

You slide open the window screen, and step inside.

Make contact with the target. Proclaim her father's
orders. But do not disclose the truth of war and politics,
for a lady made of glass and gold is far too easily broken.

Her supine body is shrouded by unnaturally long hair, and what little skin you see is the colour of polished bones in the moonlight. She does not move at your approach, or when you kneel by her side. Up close, she resembles any number of rich women in guiltless slumber.

You hate her already.

You mean to cover her mouth and shake her awake, but before your gloved hand can touch her, two black eyes snap open, a gaze sharp as fangs.

She does not scream. 'My father sent you.' Not a question. 'I knew it would happen sooner or later.'

Do not ask her why. 'Why?'

'My father delivered me to the Daimyo as collateral for his allegiance and his promise not to invade the province. And my father is not the kind of man who keeps his promises.' Her silk kimono, worth more than a lifetime of Hideo's wages, is beset by wrinkles so deep and ingrained it has warped the pattern of embroidered doves into a flock of dismembered wings. 'I suppose he's decided to invade the province after all, and has sent you to rescue me from becoming another sacrifice to his betrayals and machinations.'

That is exactly why you were sent. 'It was not put to us that way.'

'And how was it put to you?'

'We were told that your father regrets his hasty bargain. We were told he demands your safe return. We were told to come here and help coordinate your escape.'

'You were told so much and given so many words, it makes me wonder: do you have any of your own?' Beads of sweat trail from her temple to the sharp point of her chin. 'You probably already know that in a few minutes someone will be sent to check on me, so be gone.'

You began your training at five years old, and your clan will earn three hundred bushels of rice for this assignment. Do not be thwarted by this spoilt child. 'Chiyo-dono,' you say, for they told you that was her name, 'We have taken great pains–'

'Do not speak to me of your pains, *shinobi*. I have enough of my own.' She waves you off. 'Good night. And give father my regards.'

Orders fulfilled. Nothing more to do or say. But she doesn't deserve the final word, so before you descend out of her window, tell her without bow nor backward glance, 'When the time nears, we will come for you. And you *will* be ready.'

Obtain her cooperation. Ensure her strict obedience. And do not let her depart from your control, for an ally with their own agenda is quickly made an enemy.

The air turns sharp. Cicada skeletons and leaf litter spiral down from the sky, the perennial death dance of Autumn.

You sleep in a windowless, suffocating room. You partake of your meals at a crowded table tucked out of sight from your betters, a dinner of scraps where the gossip is more sustaining than the food:

Recently, the Daimyo's hostage has begun doing what she has never done since entering the castle.

She leaves her room.

Daizou wanders to the lower servants' dining room, belching loudly. 'Her kimono hasn't been washed in ages, and I hear she refuses to go to the baths or set her hair.' He looks disgusted. 'I wouldn't touch her if she were laid naked over a platter of rice.'

Agreement ripples. But that will not stop every one of them from jockeying for a single glimpse, panting after her unkempt kimono or the long, bedraggled train of jet black hair. 'What do you think, Hideo? Is she a rose or a thorn?'

Give nothing away. Earn their laughter and contempt, as only Hideo can. 'What does it matter to me? I'm not good enough for either!'

Push away your bowl. Your appetite is gone. It is gone the next day, and the next. You sleep less and less. Some nights you think you can smell the ocean. Some nights, you dream of nooses woven from strands of pitch black hair.

One afternoon in a narrow corridor, sunshine slanting over her pallid face and a retinue at her heels, she passes by you, or rather Hideo, a man who may be stupid, but not stupid enough to look a lady in the eyes.

Halt. Bow. Pray that she has more sense than manners.

Her greeting isn't much, a simple nod and, 'Hello.'

It is enough. Her string of servants and their lingering gaze brush over you one by one, paint you with a hue of newfound suspicion.

That night, you hasten back to her room. 'Do you have a death wish?'

She rests her chin over her drawn up knees, looking bored enough to be dead. 'As a child, I poked hornet nests with my bare hands. They swelled up like this.' She forms a large circle with her hands.

Do not tell her she is a fool. But make sure she knows it. 'You are under lock and key, guarded by a thousand of your enemies' eyes. There are greater risks at play than a wasp sting.'

'Such as?'

'Such as–' Stop. Tilt your head to the wall. Listen. Listen again.

A threat approaches. A heavy gait advancing from the other side of the shoji screens. You place a hand over her lips, a *kodachi* blade halfway unsheathed. 'Don't move.'

They stop outside her room. 'Chiyo-dono?'

She lowers your hand and frees her voice. 'Don't worry, Hitori-san. I'm still here. I'm always here.' A grunt, a trudge of departing footfalls, and you are alone once more with her saw-toothed comments. 'Next time, don't be so dramatic. They do that every hour, but are too lazy to come inside.'

'Your servants?'

'My prison wardens. If I go missing at any point they'll meet the same fate as the hens on a banquet day. So they like to be assured I'm still locked in my coop.' She looks at you shrewdly. 'Not all of us can come and go as we please.'

Do not rise to her bait. 'If you must know, I'm forbidden to leave the castle until my mission is over.'

A rustle of amusement in her eyes. 'Then we must be more alike than I thought.'

Tell yourself you are nothing alike. Tell yourself that her mother and father never scoured the dirt for a lost grain of rice, boiled bark and pinecones till they were soft enough to chew but not enough to digest, or buried a new child every winter. Tell yourself she could never understand how survival is warfare, and now warfare has become your only means of survival.

But do not tell her any of that. Instead, whisper, 'Never speak to me in the open again,' and fly back out of the window.

Stop. Slow down your breath. You are not being strangled, and these walls are not made of wood and stone. They are fragile as blown glass, a glass as fine and delicate as the wind chime dangling from her window, painted with cobalt waves. Attached to the fluttering wind catcher is a note addressed to

no one –

Did you know you are the first person I've ever spoken to without permission? My father hires people like you for your cunning and deceit. Honourless, that's what he calls you. I would believe him if he ever told the truth.

Take it with you. Throw it into the fire.

Do not think of it again.

Wait upon our signal. Leave no evidence behind.
And do nothing in haste or anticipation,
for a servant who has something to hope for
also has something to hide.

Rumours of espionage grow like the stack of hidden letters that live in a forgotten alcove, beneath a loose floorboard, covered by an encrusted chamber pot that only you are degenerate enough to touch.

No one will find them. Your mission is far from compromised, and you take pride in that you only read them once per day, and only at night, where her *kanji* are small and precise in the yellow corona of illicit lantern light. Her last note was an elaborate tangle of clouds and wings and flying, all the things you are trained to never think upon, and which make you accuse her of being a foolish girl who must fancy herself a very fine bird, indeed.

Her response:

A bird? Hardly. I eat birds, and would rather not chance becoming another's supper. But what could be more free than the sun?

The sun, you write in return, *which no one can touch or even look upon without getting burned. Now who does that resemble?*

She is not the only one with whom you exchange arcane messages. Many snakes have slithered into the bed of the enemy. The farmers who deliver produce each morning. The minstrel who performs each night. You may be the eyes and ears, but they are the mouth, and just as you provide them maps, the times, names, faces, weaknesses – they provide you with ever fresh and exacting orders.

At sundown, on your way back from dumping the last of the refuse over the walls, you reach your hand into a high knot in an old oak tree, in the very back of the gardens where only squirrels and rabbits roam, and withdraw a letter with a single word:

Soon.

Stop. Remember who she is. Remember where you are, and why, and the heavy price to pay when disloyalty is paired with poverty. Climb to her window, as you've done too many times before. Leave behind your master's order – the last word she will ever receive from you.

'Leaving so soon?'

You've tarried too long at her window. The wind chime sings as a slim arm glides through the open shoji screen and grasps the note. She unfolds, and reads. 'I see.'

'No more communication.'

'Or what?'

You do not know where she hides her letters, and you will never ask. 'Or you will give us away.'

'*Us*? Are we an *us* now? I don't even know your name, or where you come from.' She laughs. 'Where do you come from? North, south, east, west?'

Say nothing. She does not need to know. 'From the heart of the island. From the high mountains where nothing grows, and so no Daimyo has come to rule over us.'

'And the women there – what do they do? Do they fight like you? Are they free to do whatever they may, no matter what their fathers say?'

'In my village there are women who fight. There are women who work and women who farm and women who raise a clutch of children. There are men who do just the same, and every last one of them is poor. We do what we do because we must, because hunger is as much a prison as walls of wood and stone.' Do not indulge the memories she's aroused, threadbare images of your parents, the scent of mountain peaks and ancient trees and the misting sighs of Mount Gozaishu, and for the hundredth time stop wondering, 'How much longer?'

They told you:

You will stay however long it takes.

'No one who lives there is free,' you say.

A smudge of long black hair and dirty kimono. A wry and radiant whisper drifting to your hovering ears:

'Who is?'

Protect the target with your life. Deliver her to her father. And do not falter in any one of these points, for the shinobi who fails his mission dishonours us all.

It is Winter in Mikawa province, the seventeenth year of Tenbun, a time of snowfall and siege.

Midnight launches a foul breeze from the North, and an army of black-clad warriors over the walls of Kashigawa castle. There will be death tonight, and not only among the Daimyo's garrison.

'Goodbye, Hideo.'

Put the servant to death. Bury him with the others. Close your eyes and picture the battle joined, just as you were taught. First, the unsuspecting guards, red smiles across their throats. Next, the burgeoning fear of the gatekeepers, a grapple of flesh and steel. Finally, the lumbering grind of the rising castle gate, the flood of armoured samurai rushing into the courtyard to defend what is already lost.

Arm yourself. Count out the minutes. Five before the alarm is raised, seven before the counter-attack is organized, and a full ten before the castle is smoked with enough confusion for you to slip into her room unopposed.

You know she will not come with you. She will not return to her father. She will drive herself into your sword or fling herself off the castle walls.

Maybe you will jump after her.

Stop. Remember who you are. You know thirty kinds of inescapable knots, recipes for sleeping draughts and how to force them down uncooperative throats, the exact place to strike a body to render it immobile, unconscious. Any one of these will do against an atrophied prisoner of war.

But you will not do any of those things.

What you do is slide open the window screen, perch upon the sill, and say, 'You must come!'

'I won't go back to him.' Her voice has strength, but her face is smeared with tears and fear. She looks down at her hands clutching a thin blade. 'They call this an honourable death. Do you believe that?'

No. Or do you? What do you believe? It's been so long. So long. Beliefs, like plants, dry and crumble if left untended. 'You will never see your father again.' Walk inside. Kneel beside her. 'But only if you come!'

The blade falls to the floor. She holds out her hand to you.

There are three floors and numerous hallways from her room to the main gate, and you have memorized every step. But the route dictated to you months before leads straight to your masters – and her father – and with the maps imprinted in your mind you lay out a new path to take, one that runs through the hidden arteries of the castle.

'I've never been here before,' she whispers.

'Servants only.'

Most people you encounter are disoriented servants eager to avoid engagement. But a few members of the household, loyal and aggressive, meet their end by your blade, new seeds planted into your garden of victims. In one corridor, Daizou's corpse lies askew on the floor, a dagger deep in his throat. You step over his body, then over another, her hand gripped in yours. Her hair tickles your arm. More bodies. Footsteps swell up and down the stairs. Bodies of samurai and ladies. Ponds of slick blood. Her breath heaves and staggers at your back. Bodies of confused peasants. Somewhere, a sharp pain. Somewhere else, a shriek, then a long wail. Bodies of allies and enemies. The air flavoured with metal and salt. Her impractical *geta* stumble around all the bodies. Bodies once chained to life. Chained by the shackles of birth.

And death? Is it a true escape? Or simply a lure into another kind of prison?

You reach the back walls of the castle. Unwrap the long rope from around your chest. Tie off a sturdy knot, and tug three times to be sure. 'Remove your shoes, but do not discard them.'

She bundles her *geta* into her draping kimono. She ties her arms around your neck, and with another rope, you tie her to yourself, and begin the long descent.

'Are you hurt?' she asks.

A fugitive arrow found a haven in your side. You don't remember when. 'No.'

Three feet from the ground, you let go. Help her to her feet. Cut through the ropes binding you together. 'Put your shoes on. Quick.'

Her soggy feet slip into the wood sandals. Snow dusts her kimono, and when she wipes it off her hand comes away red. 'You are hurt.'

Grab her arm and run. A thin trail of red blooms like red spider lilies as you tramp across the snow, away from the castle, away from the battle.

'Where are you taking me?'

Don't stop running. 'Away.'

'I don't even know your name.'

'Right now they call me Hideo.'

'And before that?'

'Before that I was Daisuke. And before that Yaori. And many others, so many others.' You stumble, fall to the ground. Try to stand.

'Stop!' She holds you down, gathers a handful of snow and presses it onto the wound at your side. 'Remember your life. You will lose it if you keep going.'

'They will come after you, after us both. There is no escape. There is war in all directions, east and west and north and south, all sides surrounded by steel. There is no escape.'

Snowflakes salt her hair. 'Then where will we go?'

'Does it matter? Leave me here. Walk wherever you may. Eventually you will meet the ocean, and maybe there you will find it.'

'Find what?'

Open your mouth. You must tell her. But the darkness you live by has come for you, and at long last you fall into its grasp, fading into nothing, into no one at all.

Tell no one your name. Tell none where you have come from. Open your eyes, and remember that we are only as free as we make ourselves.

You awaken to her voice and the scent of the ocean.

'I kept walking,' she explains.

You groan. Stretch. Push yourself up from a bed of dried grass as you have never done before: with no one to please, and your eyes to the horizon.

'What a beautiful sunrise.'

You have survived another night.

Later, she will tell you the details you can't recall. The fevered flight, the kind man with an ox cart who asked no questions. A fisherman's family has given you refuge in exchange for labour, and as winter recedes and the weather grows fine you weave a net and wade into the sea, vast and deep and unbreachable, in many ways just another kind of prison.

'But I think I prefer it to all the others,' she says. 'Do you agree?'

The water, the sand, her long strands of hair all slip through your fingers as easily as air. 'I do.'

I do.

Care Instructions for Your Cryogenically Frozen Mother

Helena Pantsis

The first time you rehearsed her death was in the midst of laughter. Everyone was outside, nighttime draped around you, clinking beer bottles and drunk on the smell of charcoal. You imagined her cold in her bed, staring upwards at nothing, her eyes pale and fishlike in death. Maybe she noticed your far off look, because she grabbed your hand then and smiled, the yellow lines in her cheeks stretching so the tubes in her nostrils danced about.

When I am under, and you miss me, trace the dry veins of your arms, pretending they are mine, nostalgic for the warmth and the eternal blood flow.

It visited you in a dream once, the cold, still, breathless body, poised beside you with flesh still so young, when you pinched it, it bounced right back.

Speak of me in the present tense, with the knowledge I am merely sleeping; tell your lovers I'm unreachable, but not neglectful, and I will meet them when my flight comes back around.

When she first told you she was sick, what you heard was that she was dying. Still, it wasn't until she told you she was dying that you started to mourn her life. They used phrases like "palliative care" and "end of life plan" to describe her due course, the thing that would become her, or the things that would be taken away from her.

You have never seen a frozen lake, nor a ground of powdered snow as long as I have raised you, so you don't understand the yearning for the cold. Go far, make tracks, see your feet in the path you have walked and know the joy the frostbite brings – the land freezes over and thaws as beautiful as it once was.

The first time your mother made a decision about her care, you were stunned silent.

Take what you want from my belongings, and write to me often for the living I've missed.

'Cryogenics?'

Photograph the changes, the sunsets and the growing, the children you may have that may one day be my own.

The term was unfamiliar to you, but soon it became a promise – that the frozen, still heart would not mean death. It was a choice to delay the inevitable, your mother preserved until a cure could be found for the thing that was eating away at her. You thanked God for some reason, as if you believed in that sort of thing.

I have known nothing but cold since the illness set in, and I have been home – still, knit me blankets to make the transition easier, for when I finally wake up again, if I do wake up again before you've left this earthly plain.

Over the life of the illness you took your mother to the doctor and waited by her side as they poked and prodded and maimed and massacred her. Your mother loved telling the doctors that as a child you would punch holes in as many pieces of white paper as you could find, scattering the scraps around the floor of her room, so at Christmas time she'd be reminded of home. Your mother loved that story, telling it over and over even as she lay in the cryogenic chamber.

If I revive an old woman, rub my feet and count my medicines, put one sugar in my tea and sit me by the open porch light at night. If you overtake me, I will do the same for you. And if you pass along, please promise to haunt me, my dear.

In the days leading up to it, you would lay beside her in bed, holding your breath and forgetting to blink so you could spend as much time as you possibly could before she slept an ageless sleep. You would count the years in lieu of sheep, watching them jump over half-built houses and burying into your bones. You wondered how much you would age by the time she woke again, if you would be the same age as her, or older still.

When you feel far from me, remember I am lying here in wait of a cure, the same as if I was sleeping in my own bed. The cold doesn't exist, it is only the absence of heat. Visit the land where I was born in the winter, where your grandparents raised me – learn to ski, and build snowmen, and sled down Beacon hill. Skate on slivers of blades along the lake I did when I was growing.

There were remnants of her in the crevices of grout on your bathroom floor. You wiped a feverish brow, scrubbing the floor of sick and spontaneously welling up at the memory of it; her body hunched over the bathtub, thin and waning, grey and bent so her spine revealed itself as half a zipper.

The one thing they always forget to tell you when you put your skates on for the first time is what I'll pass on to you: the ice may be thin, may crack in the middle, and you may keep to the thick edges to avoid the drowning, but the lake is melting anyway. No matter how careful we are, one of us will eventually fall in. Make plans, my love.

Vacuum sealing the belongings she'd left in your home, you found a letter in her jacket addressed to you, the jacket she had handed you before stripping down to nothing, her body an echo of the thing it once was. You didn't read it for a few years after, hoping the science would advance quick enough for only a brief stint in suspended animation. It didn't work out that way, and you supposed things never did. The one comfort you had was the knowledge that not all things frozen stay frozen.

The lake is always melting anyway.

The Last
Airport in America

Holden Wertheimer-Meier

You've run for flights countless times. Really *run*, not just that little jog to show you were trying. Full-on sprinted for flights. Races against the clock; races against unfeeling bureaucracy. C'mon, you closed the doors sixty seconds ago, I can see the plane right there, come on, what's your name, Cheryl? Cheryl, please. I have an important meeting. Cheryl? Cheryl! But Cheryl's gone and *fifteen minutes later* you watch the last flight to Williston, North Dakota take off, and with it your hopes of landing that big sale. They don't run multiple flights to Williston, why would they? You miss the one and it's your own damn fault for wanting to go to North Dakota, and by *plane*. You melt into the intentionally uncomfortable seats of Denver International, a puddle of failed capitalism, and call your boss. They yell. Call you a "mile-high dumbass". You sit there and take it. You–

You are thinking about silly things, laughable things – you'll never miss a flight like that again. Who gives a shit about *Williston*? Even the North Dakotan survivors have probably forgotten about that oily little town, if it still exists.

They are focused on the next, on the island in the ocean that couldn't be less like North Dakota if it tried. But it's better than the only other option, better than hell. Better than cooking from the inside out, better than your hair coming out in clumps, better than forgetting your own mother's name even as she writhes in pain in front of you, a mirror of your agony as your memory fades faster than your body. You've heard those stories, and you believe them. You've read the papers, during the brief window when they still printed them. You've even seen some shaky cell phone videos, back before the internet went dark, and they gave you nightmares. That's not an end you're interested in. You'll take your chances on a desperate journey to some random island meant to save everyone, but first – one last time – don't you dare miss this damn flight. Your boss can't yell at you, but this time there's a much stronger motivator. Your boss was in Amarillo visiting family and probably didn't even know the end was coming. In one instant they were turned into radioactive sludge, perhaps their last thought: *that motherfucker better hit their targets this month if they even want a hope of me approving their vacation time.*

You guess there are worse things than being yelled at by your boss.

You still wonder why the first city to go dark was *Amarillo*, yet (for now) Los Angeles is perfectly fine, days later. You're so used to information, answers, knowledge in an instant. Not knowing the answers to such major questions – like, *what the hell is going on* – and minor ones – like, *why Amarillo first?* – is driving you crazy.

Focus.

You look up at the departure board out of habit. This is your umpteenth time in LAX so it's muscle memory, but, of course, the board is completely blank. This is the last flight out of the last airport in America, where else would you be headed? The steady march of cities going silent has almost reached the Pacific; get off this goddamn continent *today*.

You run faster.

You run past the discarded luggage, thrown open, shirts and bras and manilla envelopes full of pictures and memories, scrapbooked across the floor like a mosaic. They announced six hours ago, military guys with big bullhorns driving down the street, that you couldn't bring any luggage on the remaining flights, which didn't bother you – the only things on your wall were the first dollar you ever made, a dead spider, and a picture of your mom, who hated you anyway.

You run past the empty ticketing desks, the ones still getting electricity just blinking the words "PROCEED TO SECURITY". You used to flirt with the ticketing agents to get upgrades, regardless of gender. It never worked in fifteen years, but you kept trying. Maybe you'd grow sexier with age, you thought, but all you had to show for it was a few additional missed flights, a lifetime of coach, and one restraining order.

You run past – a body. Don't think about that. An airport employee. Don't look! Why would an airport employee shoot themselves? They knew better than anyone that there was hope just a few halls away. Unless they knew–

No, stop. Stop that thought. Focus. Run.

Security is abandoned. Not a good sign. Goddammit, you can't be too late. You look around at the TV screens to see if any of them have the time, but they're all static or blue-screened government messages. Your phone is long dead. Despite your grandfather buying you a watch every Christmas, you never wore one. You bet he made it to safety.

Your grandfather was a stubborn old sonofabitch, and he had no shortage of watches.

If it's later than midnight you're fucked, so you better run. What masochist scheduled the last flight at the end of the world for midnight like a melodramatic Bond villain?

Normally you'd be thrilled to be in an airport this empty, but today it's a horrific omen. If you're the only one running for this flight, you aren't just late, you're the *latest*. You should have stayed in better shape. Then you could have run to LAX from the hotel you were sheltering in, not walked. Or at least rode a stolen bicycle without getting winded. After the final announcements, people ran and biked past you for hours and hours on end and you felt like the most unqualified person at the marathon, until nobody was passing you and the city was silent. Surely you weren't the slowest person left in California. Unless those slower had decided not even to try. Driving wasn't an option; even at the end of the world the traffic in LA was horrible. Except those cars would never move again, long abandoned by their desperate drivers, who, like you, chose travel by foot when the call went out to head, at all costs, to Los Angeles International.

Finally, a person. Older. Alone, looking out a window.

Run, they say, You haven't missed it yet.

Aren't you coming?, you ask.

Do you know where you're going?

The island, the island on the news.

Which island?

I don't know.

Nobody does, they say with a look out the window, and a deep sigh. I keep seeing shooting stars. Or, I'm telling myself they're stars. I'm going to sit here and wait for one to reach me. I'd rather be suddenly gone than fall into the sea, know-ing the end is coming.

You look at them, speechless.

An island, they scoff. How do you hide an island for that long? Then they smile: Go. You'll miss your flight.

That's when you hear, finally: other people! Thank God. Of course, they're going to help us, the government, fully controlled by the party you voted for your entire life, you trust them. They wouldn't have started this three-day war without a backup plan, a fail-safe. The island was top secret for decades so that it could be waiting for us when we needed it, like we do now. A new Eden, the news said. You leave the pessimist to their shooting stars and keep running.

Around the corner and you're at the gate, the final gate, and you can see the lights of one of those two-story planes through the terminal window. Wings longer than most en-tire aircraft. Lie-flat seats. An international airline's artwork dancing across the side. Solid, steady, and *present.* It's before midnight. The plane is here. The gate is open. You made it.

But this is too many people. You've flown enough to know that there's never this many people at the gate, even for a big-ass plane like this one. Fuck. But this isn't Williston you'll miss if they're overbooked, one last time. This isn't a sales quota. This is your life.

You push.

You push.

You push and push

And push and push and PUSH

A mother screams, a baby cries, you knock over someone with a yelping guide dog, you step on a flight attendant's leg, but you are the crowd now. As a police officer shouts, there is room for everyone, there is room for everyone, form a line, stay calm – *you* become *we*, and we are getting on this goddamn flight.

We make one last push and the flight attendants barricading the jet bridge, the officer shouting orders, the weak among us, fall to the ground. We run, the metal of the jetway ringing out as the unlucky fall to the side, or are thrown, or fall to the pinging gunshots. An attendant is trying to close the door of the plane, but it was never meant to close in a hurry – and we are in a hurry. We spill onto the A380, punching and kicking and hitting for a seat, and it is strangely quiet as few among us shout, the only sounds the pandemonium of bodies in motion and contact and injury and death, but no real screams of anger. It's the end of the world, and we are the ones who are running late. Accepting our fate is not difficult when we are trampled underfoot, thrown from the jet bridge onto the taxiway, knocked unconscious by a beverage trolley battering ram. If we cared about our fate, we would have left the continent earlier. There were flights for two days. Every one of us has a reason for being late. And so, the screaming is minimal. It is a silent ballet of violence, of bodies, a dance to push away death for at least a few more hours, because what else can we do?

We can't help but think about the cities that are still falling silent. Just this morning: Bakersfield, Palm Springs, Santa Barbara. With each hour, closer and closer to LA. *Push.*

Once the chaos ends, the strong among us shut the doors – fingers flop on the floor from the fool who tried to hold it open – and a ringleader shouts to the pilots, if they are still there, to get the hell off this continent. And, miraculously, we take off, and you don't let yourself think about what you did when you were we, as you see the ocean and the city recede below you.

You begin to relax, and a couple of volunteers do their best to clean up the aisles and remove the injured and worse. Sniffles and a sob or two break the silence but for the most part everybody seems to be remaining calm – or frozen in panic – which you're grateful for. You can almost trick yourself into thinking this is just another flight. A red-orange glow enters the plane, and you join some onlookers on the other side of the aisle to watch an oil tanker burn bright in the middle of the sea, its silent flames the only light for miles. Soon it is lost in a thick cloud of smoke, and the plane begins to shake, and the engines begin to scream. You are terrified at first, but after hours

And hours

And hours

Of the smoke and the screams and the shaking, a calm settles over you. The news did warn that there would be world-ending cloud cover, whatever that means. You relax into the turbulence and pretend you're driving down the plentifully pot-holed highway near the house you grew up in, just a wooden box at the end of a long dirt road. You learned to drive on that highway, its every bump, divot, and imperfection burned into your soul, though you hadn't thought about it in years – no, a decade, since you hadn't visited in at least that long.

You drift off to sleep and awake to murmured voices, and the pilot in the middle of a speech. You only catch something about *remaining calm*, which of course causes you to panic. A seatmate shares with you that the plane has been flying in circles for hours, and that nobody is giving permission to land because, it seems, nobody's home.

The island is a lie!, somebody shouts, and they are quickly quieted by fellow passengers.

The pilot announces that they have no choice but to turn back for LAX or risk running out of fuel over the Pacific. They couldn't find the island. You look out the windows and you can't believe how low to the water you are. You can see individual waves, taunting you, ready to welcome you.

Looking towards where you think LAX should be you see only shadows. Skyscrapers, completely darkened, peer through the black horizon. You get closer and closer but only see buildings to your right and ocean to your left. All dark.

The damn runway lights are off, someone says, the pilots can't find the airport, they shout. Then the real panic sets in. The passengers finally let loose the screams they've been holding in for hours or even days. It takes you several seconds to realize you are one of them, yelling into the uncaring air with the terror of a life seeming more meaningless by the second.

Then, in the distance, you see it – a shooting star. Then another, and another, and another. Your friend in the airport was right, you think, as you become one yourself, a star. Your stomach flies up into your throat, and your final flight becomes a comet as you rush towards the awaiting sea.

Across the country, across the world, stars fall from the sky. There was no plan. There was no Eden. There was only a desperate shot into the night, a ploy to defer panic. And so, the planes run out of fuel, the pilots run out of ideas, and the sea runs to meet us.

That night, for the first time in over a hundred years, the power goes out. First the lights of America, the hardest-hit and the hardest-hitter, but then, one by one, each country returns to a darkness unseen in millennia. Perhaps there are candles lit by survivors huddled in caves, bombed-out buildings, the wreckage of humanity. But if there are, they never get bright enough to see from far away, to be seen by each other, and so they stay isolated. Any pockets of thinking life gradually burn out with their candles, going gently into the good night.

As the years go on with nobody to name them years, the wounds begin to heal.

Blackened craters grow weeds and moss, surrounded by toxic aquifers. But nature is patient, and the weeds and moss grow to love the taste of rare elements.

Those same craters soon become dry valleys. Something a bit like lizards, snakes, and rodents begin to emerge and squeeze what sustenance they can from the wasteland.

Most do not make it. Most.

In the surreal ruins of cities, steel girders are perfect stakes upon which the fruit of the new world can grow. Crumbling concrete allows the grandchildren of birds to build nests, and the hardiest of mammals to seek shelter from the poison air when a thunderstorm rolls in.

Each cycle of thunder, lighting, and acid rain cleans the surface, until animals begin venturing outside, begin grazing, begin hunting, begin mating.

Trees finally begin to reach unimpeded towards the empty sky, until they are taller than the last remaining buildings, the planet's newest and original skyscrapers.

Perhaps some of those that begin to make a new life on this healing world are human, but if they are, you would not recognize them as such.

As the Earth builds scars like mountains, the sea is busy. If ten thousand years after you fell from the sky, you were to walk down to the sea where the elite used to play, and peer into the waters where you screamed out your final breaths, you might see it. You'd have to wait for night, which means likely enduring the daily fall of ash, like snow. Snow in Los Angeles! Falling upon the lonely beaches, falling upon the

Hollywood hills where a species once brought their night-mares to life, falling upon the dark waves, where the last flight out of America landed. If you were to dive beneath those waves, you'd see the remains of your plane glow with a heavenly blue light, luminescent life spreading across each engine part, each piece of fuselage, and across the last physical remains of a long-forgotten species. And all the time ash falling, falling, falling, there, right there, where you died and where now stands one of thousands of coral reefs lining the coasts of a planet exploding with life.

Margins of Snow

Brigitte de Valk

Snow fell silently, each flake a little white lie. She perched on the windowsill, one ankle crossed over a knee. A thin breeze whistled through a crack in the pane. Jaqueline didn't notice. The sky outside was a wet, black brushstroke. Her fingers fumbled in a glass jar, brushing against the silken skin of cherries. She pinched one and drew it forth. Each cherry was a tiny fragment of a heart, cut out of some greater being. Her mother had been dead for weeks.

In a ritualistic fashion, Jaqueline placed the preserved fruit on her tongue. She swallowed, delicately, without a change in her facial expression. She continued to watch the snow. The lights in the garden were positioned at odd angles. Pale flurries revealed themselves, like faces appearing suddenly below the surface of a lake. She was meant to be studying. Her books lay abandoned. A ribbon of thought capered through her mind. It touched upon her recollections of that one, most significant night. It tied itself up into a complicated knot, and then fell apart. Jaqueline sighed. She tightened the lid of the jar. There was nothing more she could have told the police.

Invisible clouds shifted. Moonlight drooped like an ill lily. Jaqueline surveyed the dark. She wanted to measure the infinitesimal differences of the shadows. Memories tried to mushroom, there, in the depths of her unconscious. She wiped her fingertips on the hem of her trousers. It was best not to reminisce. Jaqueline swung her legs off the sill. The tart flavour of cherries lingered in her mouth. Her bare feet touched the hard cold of the floorboards. The thought of going to sleep was unbearable. Her dreams tended to dovetail into non-explicit dread.

Jaqueline sat at her old, wooden desk. Papers lay scattered over its surface. Words, written hurriedly, sloped across a page. She was writing a thesis on the slender spaces of white interspersed between lines of poetry. Jaqueline imagined her body reclining, corpse-stiff along brittle font, the uneven appendages of letters sticking into her spine. The foot of letters millimetres from the tip of her nose, the underbelly of *g* gently pinning her down. Those mausoleums of white space were the perfect hiding place.

Jaqueline lifted a porcelain cup of coffee to her lips. It had a gilded rim, slightly chipped. The liquid was cool and bitter. It was inevitable that conflict would occur, between the vast wasteland of a page and those vulnerable notes of ink. Jaqueline turned a page in a slim volume of poetry. Margins loomed imperiously on either side of neat, anxious quatrains. The book smelt of must. Jaqueline's pen scratched against paper. Fatal knife wounds, like dark commas, punctuated her mother's body. The corpse was found at a quarter-past midnight. Her skin had turned a pale sheen of blue. Jaqueline's pen paused. Its nib hovered above the page, sniffing the blank expanse. Under the fine grains of cellulose fibres, it searched for the next word it would form.

Jaqueline's mind became drowsy. Her eyes followed the beguiling patterns of snow, falling, falling behind her window. Frost formed like a second skin over the glass. Letters reclined and swayed on the page in front of her. Jaqueline drifted off, her neck caught at an odd angle. It would throb bitterly when she awoke.

Cylindrical boles of aspens reached up, as though they were born with a desire to cleave the air. They were single-mindedly vertical. Their trunks were nobbled with patches of black, which stuck out sharply against their bleached bark. Jaqueline wandered between them. A late afternoon sun coolly filtered between their frail branches. Her boots made thick prints in the snow. Clouds of breath formed inches from her mouth. She made this short pilgrimage every other day. Her mother lived close by. It was unfortunate that she had died in the cold, and not in the confines of her two-bedroom home. The police were still unsure as to why she had exited her abode so late at night, in nothing but a thin, pink slip. Her kitchen door had been left wide open, yawning, indifferently showcasing her pots and pans to whomever happened to pass by.

A black squirrel scurried along a branch. Jaqueline flinched. Snow crunched. Her cheeks were blushed from the icy temperature. Blood ran hotly through her veins. She pressed a gloved palm against an aspen and exhaled. Police tape had cordoned off this area until recently. Jaqueline crouched and surveyed the ground. There was nothing to indicate a human had perished here. Her mother's slip had been missing a dainty, pearled button. Jaqueline had twisted it through its tiny hole many times. Her mother usually struggled with this task. The material was glossy, and her fingers were stiff with arthritis.

Snow had melted and fallen and melted and fallen many times since the murder. Spying the button with naked eyes was delusional. Jaqueline knew this. But it was criminal to do nothing. She methodically scanned the small enclosure. Occasionally a fragment of rock glinted in the light. After inspecting a fifth piece of sediment, Jaqueline sighed and stood up. The hues of the sun had deepened and were becoming obscured by thick steeps of mist. Jaqueline turned and headed home, her feet making grooves where her previous prints had already disappeared.

A pink tinge lit up the sky. Jaqueline smoothed her palm against the page. Ink smeared. She sighed, her eyes drooping. A pen slipped from her fingers. Her mother's laughter fluttered up from a memory. The final image Jaqueline had of her mother presented itself in all its humble beauty. Her mother – bent over the sink, back to Jaqueline, her hands immersed in thick soapy water. The clink of porcelain. A throwaway goodbye. Jaqueline had let the kitchen door swing behind her. The forest hadn't housed a death at that point, at least not a human one. It still seemed innocent, fertile even, in the first beginnings of winter. The leaves were all gone of course, but it felt as though they were present. The ghostly suggestion of green hung in the air as Jaqueline traipsed home.

The pen dropped to the floor. Jaqueline started. She glanced out of the small attic window. A pure white view. The sky was brightening. It was odd for her to experience such a sight. Nocturnality had infected her. The morning was a thought that she knew existed, deep inside her, but had not witnessed in such a while. She scraped back her chair. Placing a hand on the small of her back to steady herself, she stumbled over to the sill and sat down. An empty jar of cherries permeated the air with a dank sweetness. Jaqueline placed a lid over the saccharine liquid and pushed it aside. She peered outside. Her lips trembled. She covered her mouth with a hand and let out a low, dry sob.

Sound of ringing. Jaqueline lifted her head from a plush pillow. She had been moments away from sinking into an unquestionably deep sleep. She moaned. The scent of dreams, thick and languorous beckoned her. But the ringing persisted. Her eyes scanned the floor. Her satchel was vibrating. Jaqueline's eyes closed. She waited. Her limbs grew heavy. In the brief seconds she was unconscious, she was betrayed by her own mind. Jaqueline's foot missed a step, such an important step, keeping her safe from the abyss below, but she missed it and she fell, fell forward so quickly that she was awake, and the phone was still ringing.

'Hello?' she murmured. She sat on her floor. Her pyjamas were nautical, almost sailor-like. Jaqueline traced her bare foot with a finger. She was cross-legged. Her head hung forward. A voice was speaking on the other end of the line. It was baritone. The words were shapes pinned up on a line, containing meanings that dried in the wind. Jaqueline tried to catch hold of these meanings, but they rippled and flapped and besides, the line was far too high. 'Yes, I'm here.' She tried to concentrate. New evidence had been found at her mother's house. The detective explained it all to her again. She was needed for questioning. Could she get to the station, in an hour? Jaqueline nodded. Her eyelids closed. There was brief silence. 'Yes,' she said, and put down her phone.

Jaqueline blinked around her room. Sunlight tendrilled across the floorboards, forming brilliant patterns against the wood. Her bed, with its soft white duvet, and its plump, warm pillows lamented with her. Jaqueline reached for the door handle and pulled herself up. She glanced into a mirror, wincing at the reflection of bright light. Day had arrived so quickly, demolishing any notion of subtlety. She arched her back. Her wardrobe door was ajar.

Night. This was better. There was nothing more luminous than the silver glint of the moon. Jaqueline was dog-tired but couldn't sleep. She sat at her desk and poured herself a fourth cup of coffee from the decanter. She pressed the tips of her fingers together and bowed her head, as though praying. Her mouth was dry. She was reliving the day, question by question. Sweat had dampened and then dried into the underarms of her shirt, leaving the material coarse. Jaqueline remained in her shirt, although it was unbuttoned now, and her suit trousers had been tossed to the floor. Goose-pimples formed along her legs. She ignored the cold. She inhaled through her nose and picked up her pen. She wrote one last question on the page in front of her. On the floor were reams of paper, covered in the black ink of her answers. Verbatim. Jaqueline had an excellent memory. Empty cartridges lay scattered on the ground, like insignificant, crushed insects. It hurt to wrap her fingers around her fountain pen. The insides of her fingers were lightly bruised. She had been writing for hours.

Jaqueline frowned. The detective had stared into her eyes so deeply, it was as though she had wanted to peel back the glint of her irises. Photographs of her mother had been presented, which Jaqueline thought was cruel. So much tenderness in her mother's expression, even in death. Snow began to fall, each flake a pearlescent button, waiting to be swallowed. Her replies had been elegantly uttered. There were enough subtle hesitations for verisimilitude, and the skin of her lip had broken, as if on cue. The detective had passed her a tissue, to stem the droplets of bright blood. Jaqueline hoped sympathy had been conjured at that moment. Shedding tears seemed too obvious a gesture. Painstakingly, she had held them back, her gaze darting around the perfectly square room, with its empty corkboard and mismatched chairs.

The nib of her pen snapped. It was as if a bone had broken. Jaqueline shook her head. Her throat was parched. She touched it gently. They had offered her numerous plastic cups of water. The thin plastic crackled each time she lifted it to her lips. She could tell it disturbed the detective, a middle-aged woman with deep, oceanic pupils. Can you recount, can you recount, she asked. Do you recall, do you recall? The window behind her brightened and busied with clouds. Jaqueline had painted her mother's toenails the night before her murder. She lacquered the tiny brush with a soft fawn and delicately applied it. Her mother's breathing soon calmed. It was an intimate moment between them, where words were not necessary. The detective rifled through her files and pushed an image of her mother's feet across the table. Ankles-up, she was covered in a white sheet. Jaqueline surveyed the minute areas in which the polish overspilled onto skin.

Jaqueline's phone screen was dark. It had run out of battery. She had no intention of charging it. The police would call again. They hadn't revealed the new evidence to her. Perhaps they would on her next visit. Jaqueline was adept at unlocking secrets. Her mother could keep nothing from her. She raked a hand through her hair. Almost instinctively, she glanced towards her drawers, where her mother's diaries lay hidden among folded clothes. It was unnecessary to keep them in a secure place. Nobody would come looking here anymore.

A sharp little pain pinpricked her stomach. Closing her eyes, she felt her way to her bed.

If she squinted, the spaces in the poem were white petal pulp. Slender cloaks of invisibility. Tunnels of diffidence, where she could lay her little finger, without obscuring the words above or below. She loved the thought of cleanliness. It didn't transpire often in her real world. The contents of her room were lovingly embraced by dust, and her pile of cups clattered if she dropped something heavy to the floor. Jaqueline imagined pulling and tugging on the membranes of her thoughts until they were amorphous and could be re-moulded into poetic sentiments. But she was not a poet. She was a scholar. Her mind analysed and critiqued. She tore open sentences and found suggestions, carefully concealed. Now, she was determined to infuse those pauses with meaning. Every mind translated the glimpse of page as silence, but it didn't have to be that way. Jaqueline locked her hands together and stretched.

The taut stomach of the sky had been cut. Out whirled multitudes of flakes. A carousel of white derailed outside her window, so that its ice-horses cantered wildly, nostrils flaring. Soon there would be a thick layer of snow upon the ground. It was useless to procrastinate. The same academic work would haunt her tomorrow. There was a particular poem her mother always recited. Her lips formed each word, haltingly. Jaqueline would not so much listen to the words, as watch the subtle expressions ripple across her mother's face. There was a line, somewhere tucked into the last stanza, which caused the world to disappear. Her mother became blind to her child's room, and saw only inwardly, to some distant isle of desire. Jaqueline always held her breath at this moment. The reverie soon ended and so did the poem.

Jaqueline tousled her hair. Her concentration waned. From a fresh, sharp nib, a triplet of blackbirds blossomed, ricocheting across the bottom of the page. Their wingspan was minute and decreased further as each new bird was born. The youngest was merely a malignant mole, seeping into the paper, faintly staining the next page.

The grove of aspens called softly. Perhaps to one another. Perhaps to the pale eye of the sky that dewed then cleared then dewed again. Finally, a thin gauze of clouds covered its gaze.

Outrunning the Bear

Liz Ulin

There he is, slipping out from behind the pines,
hunting me.

I drag my legs through deep snow, sweat blooming,
glance back, tamp down the panic.

His grisly snout sniffs the frigid air, huffing steam.
We lock eyes. A low rumble rises from his chest.

Christ, he's close today.

Generally he just makes an appearance,
lets me get a whiff before lumbering off.

He'll snap a twig underfoot, rustle some bushes –
practised power moves.

Stalking ladies of a certain age,
an easy form of entertainment.

For most of my life he's been a lazy bear,
lucky for me.

When I was a child, he kept his distance,
deep in the forest, disguised as a regular creature.

Content to forage for other flesh:
salmon or blueberries, presumably.

In adolescence, he finally caught my scent, his tastes evolving.
Some light mauling, the predictable result.

Though, at the time, the chase could be perversely thrilling,
if I'm being honest.

But as I grew smaller, and ever less defensible,
the bear embraced his beastly nature, turning to serious business.

Once, in the turquoise sea off Cozumel, he nearly had me.
Far from shore, his claws at my ankle, tugging me under.

The distant sunbathers too tiny, the gulf too wide.
A fearsome tussle, a narrow escape.

No holiday from the bear.

At sixty-one I'm justly prudent now, but oh so bloody slow.
I hear his belly grumble and know he's good and hungry.

Today I stumble in the snow, bracing for his teeth against my neck. But minutes pass, and nothing. I struggle to my feet.

And there he is scratching his hairy pelt against a tree, biding his time. It's too good a game to end today.

One of us is still having fun.

One
Flap of a
Storm Crow's Wings

Jamie Perrault

'Are we going to die?'

'No.' Algar feeds a little bit more of their dwindling wood pile to the flame. The storm may almost be over, but he has two children to keep warm, one still on the breast. Though his magic may allow him to kindle the fire again if it goes out, it costs far less wood and energy to simply keep it going.

The storm still rages outside, though the sound of lightning has become less and less frequent over the last few hours. Algar touches the pendant beneath his shirt, grateful for that bit of respite, at least. Though this is hardly the first disaster he's willingly walked into for his god, storms and the lightning-beasts that dwell inside them will always remind him of his own first home and how it was lost.

The catacomb system that Algar found to give their little group shelter has served them well for the last three days. Frigid water collects in the lowest-lying areas, but Algar's been able to keep Bernard and Corentin safe and warm on higher shelves, and there's enough ventilation for their fire to be both feasible and safe. Corentin, at least, has also been well fed, the babe continuing to suckle as though nothing untoward were happening.

As if sensing Algar's thought, the baby starts to squirm. They don't quite work themself up into a proper fuss, but Algar doesn't intend to give them time to do so.

Unclasping his tunic, Algar pulls out his right breast and shoves it into the babe's mouth. Corentin immediately latches, beginning to suckle happily, their little hands kneading the flesh.

Bernard watches, his face twisting with the same confusion it has every time Algar has done this. Now that the storm's abating, Algar can spare enough energy to prod the boy's curiosity.

'You can ask me, you know.' Algar keeps his voice gentle.

Frowning, the boy takes one of the smouldering sticks from the fire and pokes it into brighter, sparking life for a moment. 'You said your name's Algar, and your hair is cut like a boy's, but you... uh... you're a mother?'

'Nope, I'm a father.' Algar smiles to take any sting out of the words. 'You don't have anyone here like me?'

Bernard shakes his head, then pauses. 'Not that I know of, at least. I wouldn't have guessed about you if you weren't... you know.'

'I do.' Algar kisses his child's head, smiling at the feel of wispy baby hair against his face. None of them smell terribly great, not after three days cooped up in here, but Corentin's skin still gives off an unmistakable aroma that Algar could breathe for ages. 'I'm just a wanderer, doing my best by me and my family.'

Bernard's face immediately turns towards the opening in the catacomb system. 'Do you think my family...'

'I think they'll have done their best.' Algar moves a little closer to the boy, though he doesn't reach out to touch him. 'We'll see soon what's become of everyone.'

'I want them all to be fine.' Bernard swallows hard, his eyes slick with unshed tears. 'I want everything to be just the way it was, but… it's not going to be, is it?'

'No.' Algar keeps his voice gentle, but he won't try to hide this truth. Eight is young to learn it, but Bernard undoubtedly sensed from the moment Algar plucked him out of the raging river that had replaced the quiet stream he knew so well that nothing remains the same in the face of a storm like this. 'There will be damage and loss. But there will also be opportunities, and reunions. Don't worry until we see exactly what's happened.'

'I don't understand *why*.' Abandoning his stick, Bernard hugs his knees to his chest. 'Why did this have to happen to *us*?'

'Why not you?' The boy has leaned closer, so Algar reaches out to put a hand on his head. He's not surprised when Bernard leans more heavily against him. 'Would you wish it on someone else, instead?'

The boy thinks for far longer than most adults would. '…would I be a bad person? If I said yes?'

Algar can feel where tears are soaking through the side of his tunic, but he doesn't betray the boy by looking to confirm that they're his tears, slipping free of a child's control. 'You wouldn't be a bad person for wishing it. Nobody wishes to suffer, but storms come through everyone's life. What makes you a bad person is if you're willing to steer storms towards others that you could weather yourself, or that nobody has to weather at all.'

'There wasn't any warning!' Bernard's whole body shivers, his righteous child's fury at the unfairness of the world breaking through. 'If there was warning we could have moved the livestock, and fortified the houses, and– and stood a *chance*. But instead... are all my sheep going to be dead? Lefty just had lambs, and Gorger was due... are they all going to be dead?'

'I don't know.' Algar touches the pendant around his neck once more – the tree with bare branches and an intricate root system. 'No one knows until it's over. Animals have their own sense of what to do in a storm, and they'll have tried to get to high ground. We'll know who survived and who didn't soon, when the rain finally stops.'

Bernard doesn't say more, just allowing Algar to stroke his hair.

Algar keeps the fire going through the rest of the storm, until the patter of water outside their catacomb safety has finally dissipated, and they can emerge to see what's become of Bernard's home.

The people of Kavashil welcome Algar with open arms despite all that they've suffered. Algar recognizes the hurt they're facing – the houses that have flooded, the ones that have collapsed, the handful that burned when lightning took root before water could extinguish. They are new images that rest atop old ones, and Algar knows what to do to try to help these people.

He's lived through something like this once already, after all, and he didn't even have his pendant or his magic or his god then.

They trust him almost immediately, which is a nice change from some places Algar has been called to. He appears carrying one of their thought-lost children in his arms, after all, and that inclines them to trust the knowledge he has – the knowledge that will help them rebuild.

In return for his assistance, Algar is given a bowl with which to scoop soup from the communal pot that is always burning, and is allowed to clean himself and Corentin with some of the boiled water that they begin crafting in big batches as soon as he recommends it.

'You've the look of someone who's been through this before.' The old woman stirring the soup studies Algar as he attempts to feed himself with one hand and soothe Corentin's angry grunting with the other. 'What kind of wanderer are you, exactly?'

Pulling his amulet out of his tunic – a move that at least temporarily arrests Corentin's attention, thank every holy entity that ever existed – Algar allows it to spin in the light. 'Do you recognize this?'

The old woman leans closer, peering intently, and then shakes her head. 'Not a bit. There are plenty of gods out there, though.'

'There are.' Dangling the pendant over Corentin distracts them enough that Algar is able to shovel several spoonfuls of soup into his mouth. He hums in pleasure at the warmth of the soup saturating his chilly body and filling his growling stomach. 'My lord is called That Which Grows from the Ashes.'

'A mouthful.' The old woman rocks back and forth, continuing to stir, the motion seeming to come to her as naturally as breathing.

Algar laughs. 'It is, isn't it? I'm assured it's less of a mouthful to the trees, and also that they are far more patient than most humans when it comes to any length of conversation.'

The woman snorts. 'You serve a tree?'

Drawing in a deep breath, Algar arranges his thoughts on the entity that has guided his steps since the loss of his home two decades prior. He's used to serving his god; he's not used to speaking about him. 'The one I serve has come to me as many different forms, but the one I see most often is a great tree, shrouded in other green growing things, that rises from a bed of ash. They bid me go where there have been... storms, and help those affected by them to regrow. The soil is often more fertile after a fire, you know?'

Bright green eyes study him from the woman's wrinkled face. 'That's a pretty way of saying you're a storm crow for your god. And that god wants you to bring a child with you as you go?'

Algar shrugs. 'Corentin is mine, a gift from another wanderer that I saved in my god's name. I could hardly abandon them while they still need my milk, could I?'

'You're a strange one, you are.' Tossing another handful of radishes into the soup, the old woman shuffles a little bit closer to the fire. 'But anyone who can work right now is welcome here, and you're doing more than your fair share.'

'I do what I can, and I appreciate your hospitality.' Algar finishes his bowl as quickly as he can, before Corentin tires of chewing on the pendant and decides they need more attention.

He will be glad enough to help as much as he's able, but he knows that there's something else he will have to do.

There always is when his lord directs him to a place like this.

Bernard is the one who brings Algar to the creature.

The boy's been out searching for his lost sheep. Though some survived, following an old ewe to a protected shelter, over half haven't. Algar doesn't know how many of the boy's tears are for the people who have been lost, the buildings, or the sheep.

If the boy is anything like Algar was at his age, it's likely Bernard doesn't know, either.

'This way.' Bernard skitters with the quick, sure steps of youth across the slippery rocks of the mountainside. 'At first I thought it was something that had fallen from the sky, but then I thought maybe it was something that had been swept down from the heavens, and then... then I realized what it must be, and knew I had to find someone who knew about...' Wiggling his fingers, Bernard casts a nervous look back at Algar.

Algar smiles, wiggling his fingers in return and sending a series of bright blue sparks into the air. The amount of strength it costs him to do showy, useless magic like that is small, and it brings a smile to the boy's mouth just as Algar knew it would.

Bernard turns back around, stopping a handful of times to look around and get his bearings. He seems more irritated each time, finally blurting out, 'It *changed* everything! Stupid, useless storm. I never would've gotten lost before. Not that we're lost now. It's just over here.'

Algar doesn't complain, merely opening his shirt and allowing Corentin to feed again. The child doesn't complain, either, glad that Algar is moving and that food is forthcoming.

Finally Bernard leads them over a little rise, and points to where an ancient tree with charred limbs has tumbled down along with a series of boulders to create a small muddy tangle. Light erupts every few seconds from the tangle, crackling and snarling in the moist post-storm air.

'No.' Algar raises his hand to the pendant around his throat. 'No, you *can't...*'

There's no answer, of course. His lord isn't one to state what's obvious.

Is Algar supposed to kill the beast? He could do that, probably. But could that possibly be what his god wants? Could that ancient, sturdy being have really brought him here for... what? Revenge?

'It *is* something magical, isn't it?' Bernard presses up against Algar's right side. 'What is it? Sometimes it looks like a fox, and sometimes like a rabbit, and always it's giving off that yellow stuff that feels... tingly when I get too close.'

'Lightning. It's giving off lightning.' Algar begins undoing the straps that keep Corentin tight against him. His arms feel distant and strange, too long for his body. 'You've heard of storm dogs?'

Bernard's eyes widen, and he takes a step towards the beast. 'That's a storm dog?'

'Yes.' Algar steps forward as well, not wanting to let the boy closer to the storm dog without protection. The ground seems to pitch beneath him, the earth as unstable as the sea.

That's a dangerous thing to think, in this place where the ground has clearly become loose and fractious from the storm. Placing a hand on Bernard's shoulder, Algar makes sure the boy won't go any closer, while using the boy's breaths to slow his own. When he speaks, his voice is far calmer than he would have expected. 'I've seen the storm dogs before, when my home town burned.'

The storm dogs danced, then, a swirling, twirling mess of white and yellow creatures that flitted from rooftop to rooftop and left fire and destruction in their wake. Algar hadn't even seen ten summers, but he'd helped with a dozen failed bucket brigades before the night was over.

Algar dreamed of his god for the first time when he finally tumbled into an exhausted sleep, his arms still twitching with the motion of filling and passing the bucket.

Bernard's hands clench into tight fists. 'Then– then did it *cause* the storm? Did it–' The boy's words trail off into spitting, soundless rage.

'No.' Algar reminds himself of that as he cradles Corentin close and kisses their head. 'Storm dogs ride the storms, and they bring lightning, but they don't form the storm. Not unless there are hundreds of them. Perhaps if something disturbed a nesting ground... but even then, it's not the storm dog's fault. They're magic, but they're not gods or anything. They just... are, like a wolf is.'

'I attack wolves that try to go after my sheep.' Bernard's jaw stays set.

Disengaging Corentin from his breast, Algar hands him to Bernard, forcing the boy to unclench his hands if he doesn't want to drop the child. 'Keep them safe, all right? I'm going to go see what can be done.'

Bernard looks up at him with wide, wondering eyes. 'Can you kill it, then? Is that what you're going to do?'

'I'll let you know as soon as I'm certain.' Tying his shirt back into place, Algar begins his approach of the fallen creature.

The storm dog snarls as soon as he gets close. The creature's fur is beautiful, a creamy colour that seems to bend like waves in a storm as the lightning that would usually keep it up among the clouds courses over its body. It's obvious even from a distance why the creature didn't leave with the storm. One of the tumbled rocks has pinned it, and though he can't see for certain from any safe angle Algar thinks a branch of the great tree might also have impaled the beast.

'Did you bring this on yourself, then?' Algar's words would likely sound calm to any outsider, but Algar can hear the tremble in them. 'Did you dive down to strike that old tree, and bring yourself to ruin in the process?'

The storm dog doesn't answer. It's not a person, after all. It, like the storm, is not responsible for the destruction it brings.

Lifting his pendant free of his tunic, Algar studies the slick dark metal. 'I didn't think there were any tests you had left to give me, but that's why you're a god and I'm a mortal, I suppose.'

There's no answer. There very rarely is, not to direct provocations like that.

Allowing his pendant to dangle down in full view, Algar begins preparing what he'll need for his ritual. The herbs he needs are in his pack, and they catch fire readily despite the damp ground all around them. The sigils he needs are burned into his memory, years of study and use having made them second nature.

The calm... ah, that's something that he has to provide himself, and it takes him longer than it should to settle into a proper meditative space.

Once there, he can feel the power of the storm dog – feel what it *should* be, and see what it is. The beast has been badly hurt. The easy thing – perhaps the proper thing – would be to grab what is left of its energy and dissipate it out into the surrounding landscape. Let the body, light as a bird's, disintegrate into the soil that it burned. Let something new and precious grow from the horror that has existed here.

If that is what you wish. That Which Grows is the softest whisper in the back of Algar's mind, a comforting presence and a curious observer. *That would certainly be within the parameters of my being.*

What else would you want me to do? Algar keeps his breathing slow and even, trying to match his god's infuriating cadence.

What you think will bring the most growth from these ashes.

Algar finds his head turning, an invisible pressure like that of a hanging vine wrapped around his neck making it impossible for him to disobey.

Bernard holds Corentin close. Both child and boy have their attention fixed unerringly on where he's sitting.

Drawing in a deep breath, Algar finishes the turn, facing Bernard squarely. 'Do you want vengeance, boy? Do you want to watch this storm dog die?'

Shrinking back a step, Bernard looks from Algar to where the storm dog continues to spark. 'Why wouldn't I?'

'Because sometimes you've seen enough death. Because it isn't the storm dog's fault. Because you're a child, and people think children forgive so easily, but that isn't really the case, is it?' Algar's tongue moves too slowly, his god's touch still in his mind. 'I'm sorry. It isn't my place to ask this of you. It isn't your place to decide, and it isn't you who needs to decide if you want vengeance, not really.'

He's trying to avoid having to make the decision himself. He's trying to foist it off on someone else's shoulders – to say that the ending of the storm dog is inevitable, that it will be kindness and justice to hasten its demise.

It would be kinder than leaving it trapped here, that's true. The position that it's in is untenable.

But that doesn't give Algar the right to say that only its bones have worth now.

Sighing, Algar turns back to the storm dog. Bernard is speaking, he thinks – likely protesting that he isn't a child, and trying to elucidate whether he wants vengeance or not, when a child's hurt should never be used to justify more cruelty.

Algar would talk him through this, but Algar can't hold the human conversation in his mind right now. Not when all of his senses are slow, and open, and burning with the certainty that death is not the only possible outcome for this creature.

Do you want me to heal the creature? Algar grasps for any further guidance.

I want you to do what's best for your own healing. I want you to grow, little one.

Algar has killed before. When it's to protect himself, or others, Algar doesn't hesitate to use his magic to kill.

This would not be protection. It might be kindness, but it will be kindness only if other methods fail.

Algar wants to sleep well tonight. He wants to heal in the village without feeling this decision hanging over every moment.

There is no fault to be laid at the storm dog's feet, after all, just as there's no fault to be laid on the villagers. There are just survivors of the storm, and is it really the right of the storm crow to kill the storm dog?

Algar's magic encircles the storm dog, a pattern of blue and green energy that meshes with its yellow lightning. The storm dog tries to get away, but there isn't any escape path. If there was, it wouldn't still be here, and Algar would have no decision to make at all.

The fallen tree begins to crack, wood splinting, ashen patches crumbling to the ground. Green twigs begin to push their way up through the cracks in the bark, crawling their way towards the sun, their roots buried in the soft ash.

As the plants grow, Algar grabs their power, harnessing it to wrap around the storm dog. Willing flesh to grow, to cover the hole that the tree left behind; willing bones to knit, and even though they aren't straight, they will at least allow for movement.

The storm dog erupts out of the magic, dashing up, up, up into a cloud that had been soft and white. The cloud immediately darkens, but no rain falls, and then the storm dog is off, racing cloud to cloud, searching for the brethren that left it behind as a lost cause.

Algar sits abruptly, allowing the magic to flow out of him. His head still feels heavy, his thoughts too slow and tangled.

Bernard pushes forward, taking each step with slow, deliberate care. Only when he crosses into Algar's space without anything happening does he relax his grip on Corentin, pressing the child back into Algar's hands.

'That...' Bernard swallows. 'I've never seen anything like that. It was beautiful, and it was terrible, and... are you *sure* that was the right thing to do?'

'Not at all.' Algar begins retying the harness that will keep Corentin safely tethered to him. 'But it was kind, and I could do it, and in the wake of any storm, isn't that what we should all strive to be?'

The boy frowns, but he doesn't argue. He just sits by Algar's side until Algar is able to stand again, and then allows Algar to place a hand on his shoulder as they begin the long trek back to the village.

Bernard finds one of Lefty's lambs the next day. One leg is broken, but Algar is able to heal it with a touch.

All of the healing seems to go better, and he doesn't know if that's because the rain has seeped down as far as it needs to in order to encourage new life or if his god is pleased with him. Algar hopes it's both.

The old woman ladles soup into his bowl without having to be asked, her gaze raking up and down his body. 'You're a strange one, storm crow. Or would you prefer I call you healer?'

'Both are true.' Algar doesn't bother with utensils, just lifting the bowl to his mouth and gulping the soup as fast as he can. Corentin is currently sleeping, and he doesn't know how long that respite will last. 'So choose which one you like.'

The old woman doesn't answer, instead saying, 'You're giving Bernard ideas.'

Which is, in itself, a bit of an answer. 'Bernard will do what he's called to do – what feels right to him.'

'We've already lost plenty enough. We don't need children chasing ghost-gods and phantom monsters.' The old woman sniffs.

Algar shrugs. 'What we need and what life gives us... these aren't always the same.'

Her lips turn up into a smile. 'If he follows you, what are you going to do?'

'He's not going to follow me.' Algar speaks with absolute conviction. 'His parents are alive, and his sheep need him. But if he dreams, and if those dreams lead him to me for guidance at some distant point in the future... I won't be surprised if our paths cross again.'

Silence sits heavy between them for a few seconds before the woman says, 'Who taught you to be kind, storm crow?'

'Nobody.' Algar finishes his soup, then runs his finger around the inside to help clear it. 'I chose it, just as every other person chooses kindness or cruelty.'

'I would have thought that storms would breed cruelty.' She lifts one eyebrow in clear inquiry.

'Storms breed pain, but pain doesn't have to lead to cruelty.' Every scrap of food cleared from the bowl, Algar sets it in the pile with the others that will have to be washed. 'Pain can just as easily guide someone to want to help as to want to hurt. Surely you've seen that, teacher?'

She smiles at the endearment, though her eyes stay on the bowl rather than him. 'Are you already leaving us?'

'I've done what I need to do, and I have a husband who will likely be done with his own travels soon.' Algar can't help but grin at her startled expression. 'What, you didn't think I magicked myself up a baby, did you?'

'It wouldn't be the strangest thing I've heard lately.' Shaking her head, the old woman returns to stirring the soup. 'Safe travels, healer. I pray that our paths never have reason to cross again.'

'I pray for that, too.' Pulling his pendant from his shirt, Algar kisses the back of it before turning and heading for the edge of the ravaged village.

He's done what he can. He's given what little bits of strength and hope he has to spare. He's ensured that in this place, like in all the others he visits, something green and beautiful will have a chance to grow from the scattered ashes of broken expectations.

It's what a god once did for him, and even if his hands aren't as strong as they need to be – even if his magic isn't as certain as he hopes it one day will be – hopefully it will be enough to create more kindness than cruelty out of this latest storm.

Or Just After

Liza Wieland

Something would have to be done about the ashes. Eventually, Nisha would have to let them go. Nisha believed Djuna would want to be with Mommy and Daddy, and that meant Mumbai, but Nisha knew she could never go home again, to that home.

And yet. The idea of Djuna's ashes with her parents' ashes was becoming a kind of obsession.

Ridiculous, Michael said.

She had expected such a reaction. Ten years ago, he said her parents' ashes had been swallowed by fish in the harbour or drifted to the ocean floor or washed back in to the beach and stuck on the bottom of some tourist's sandal. Stop it, she'd told him. Stop dishonouring the dead. It's true, though, he'd said. You know it's true. He thought she'd feel less pain if she could see the situation realistically.

And now they had nearly the same conversation.

'It's a symbol,' she said, weeping. 'A metaphor. Don't you get it? My sister with my parents.'

He tried to put his arms around her, but she shook him off.

'But why does it have to be Mumbai? Can we try to find a less exhausting metaphor? A less expensive metaphor? Less dangerous?'

'You don't get it. She's not your sister.'

Michael slammed the door on his way out.

But she'd done what he suggested, planned it out differently. Less expensive anyway. She'd chosen a day: her parents' wedding anniversary, October 15. So in some way they could all be together. And she'd worked herself around to a different place. Tiny steps, nearly imperceptible realignments, exchanges, *deals*. Bargaining: it was one of those famous five stages, though she seemed to be getting them out of order. Bargaining combined with revelation: one day, Nisha woke up and knew that she wanted to have Djuna nearby, that she'd wanted this all along. Djuna in her river, in North Carolina. Djuna a mermaid, both real and not. On October 15, at noon, Sunday, Nisha would row out to the middle of the river and, drifting along toward the village, pour the ashes overboard, most of them, saving a few for herself.

As the day approached, so did Hurricane Ismene. It didn't matter. Even in the hurricane, she'd still do it, scatter the ashes. The promise of that storm on this day seemed fitting.

'Maybe it's the opposite,' Michael said. 'Maybe it's telling you not to. That it's a bad idea.'

'I don't think so,' Nisha said. 'I think it's a test.'

'The universe is benign.'

'I can't talk about this with you.'

'If you drown, you won't be able to talk about it with anybody,' Michael said. 'What about a compromise? The day after.'

'I want it to be a day that means something.'

'Stand out on the dock.'

'It's not the same.'

'You're being ridiculous.'

'*You* think I'm being ridiculous. Why can't you understand I have to do this?'

'Even if you drown?'

'Maybe I want to drown.'

This was Friday. By Saturday night, Ismene would make landfall, and Michael behind all that glass, facing into the wind off the river and the rising water. Nisha would be in the village, safe in her condo, a converted schoolhouse, far enough from the water's edge, and protected by double brick walls and the ghosts of wilful, imperious schoolteachers.

She offered to go over to the river house to help Michael bring plants inside, haul sandbags, move the cars to higher ground, even though she knew two facts. First, there was so little that could be done in preparation. It would all take about 20 minutes. Second, Michael would say yes because he wanted her company. She wondered if he was getting any better at being alone. She hoped he was, but she doubted it. So she'd asked, and he'd said yes, but that she didn't have to come over, that he understood if she felt safer where she was. Which was perhaps code for what was likely his hope: you might get stuck here.

She went, to make him happy, at least temporarily. It was a strange new power since their separation, and she hated to use it.

They stood downstairs, crowded inside the old shell of the house, surveying the jumble of their old life. It was as hideous as she remembered, one of the reasons she'd wanted to leave. Every square inch was piled with boxes of – she didn't know what anymore. Books, extra kitchen equipment, dishes, two leather couches they'd got for free from a friend, now coated with dust and probably filled with mice droppings, and maybe the mice too. Michael's tools, from tiny screwdrivers to power saws and a lathe, tucked or wedged into any open space, half of them rusted from the last two hurricanes. It looked like madness: the handiwork of a hoarder, who would perish when forty years of saved newspapers caught fire.

'I can't move it all,' Michael said. 'It's all going to get ruined. Again.'

'We bought the trailer for exactly this,' Nisha said. 'It can go in the trailer. Or some of it can.'

'The trailer is already full.'

'We don't need this stuff, Michael.'

'How do you know?' His tone was meditative, almost tender.

'It's been sitting down here for how many years now? Six?'

'I know. But I was thinking we would build that extra room. And now maybe you need...'

'My place came furnished.'

'I wondered about that.'

'We can take some of this upstairs probably.'

'But what?' He waved his arms in a gesture of frantic helplessness.

'I know,' Nisha said. 'Maybe those little boxes?'

'Your stuff.'

'I don't mean it that way.'

'What about books?'

'Books definitely.'

'But where will we put them?'

'Isn't there one more shelf in the bedroom?'

'You obviously haven't been in the bedroom lately.'

Nisha sighed. She held her tongue. She wanted to say it back to him. *Obviously*. But what would that accomplish?

'We could move some of these boxes up higher,' she said. 'In the other rooms.'

'There's no space, even Djuna's old room.'

'Don't say old.'

'What am I supposed to say?'

'I don't know. I really don't know.'

'Anyway, those shelves are packed to the gills. Every shelf in this whole goddamned house.'

Nisha knew it wasn't true. She'd taken several boxes from shelves in Djuna's room and their bedroom. There was a lot of space now. Michael must not have noticed. She didn't want to point it out.

She saw that Michael had stepped closer. She felt fear enter her heart like a needle, a cold, thin piercing. She couldn't move. He slid his arm around her waist, moved his hip against hers. She didn't know what this gesture meant or what it could become. Last weekend when she was dropping off the mail, he'd come up behind her suddenly and wrapped his arms over her shoulders, around her neck, against her throat. 'Are you trying to kill me?' she'd asked, choking out a laugh. In the moment, it had seemed entirely possible. He'd just come inside from cutting the grass and had moved toward her quickly, without saying a word.

'It's so sad,' he said now, pulling her closer. 'All this.'

'I know.' She hugged him back.

'I wish we didn't have so much shit, but we needed it all.'

'We did,' Nisha said. 'And now we don't. How does that happen? That you stop needing things?'

Michael dropped his arm and stepped away. 'I don't have a fucking clue,' he said.

What had she really meant? Nisha wondered. This was the sort of moment, a sudden mood shift when she would have exchanged a look with Djuna or moved out of Michael's reach and gone to find Djuna and hugged her or stroked her hair. That's the one thing she did need. And now Djuna wasn't there.

'Remember that time,' he said. 'I threatened to break Djuna's computer?'

'Yes.'

'I feel like I want to do it now. To get her to come back.' He said he wanted Djuna to come screaming at him through the keyboard, through the broken, separated keys, through the bedroom window, through the door. He wanted her body to come down from the bunk bed as if she'd just been asleep up there the whole time.

Later, they sat in their chairs, waiting, the lamp burning between them, the steady wind punctuated by gusts that shook the house, rattled the windows. They heard a slicing sound, and then a clatter in the yard below.

'That was a shingle,' Michael said.

'I thought so.'

'It's early to lose a shingle.'

'I wonder how long before the power... I don't even want to say it.'

'I know. Don't say it.'

'I have to admit I'm worried about the new neighbours,' Nisha said. 'They have no idea.'

Michael's expression softened, and he reached across the table between them, patted Nisha's hand. 'You're a good person,' he said.

'Thanks for saying so.'

Michael sighed, withdrew his hand. 'Why don't you believe anything I say? Jesus.'

'I didn't mean it that way, Michael. I meant thank you, that's all. Why do you assume every word out of my mouth is somehow a slight?'

'Because it usually is.'

'I don't know if I should stay here.'

'Well, you can't leave now.'

Nisha leaned back, closed her eyes. Mommy, Daddy, I need you, she thought. Why does he hate me? Make him not hate me. Or lift me out of this house and into my car and fly my car back to town where I'll be safer anyway.

Michael heaved himself out of his chair and headed into their bedroom. On the way, he banged the wall with his fist. A small voice in Nisha's head told her *go now*. Not even the words exactly, more like a convulsive gathering of viscera and will. Nisha stood up, lifted her raincoat off the peg by the door, stepped into her boots. She waited. She heard the toilet flush and the bathroom light snap off, a sound like a dry cough.

When he saw her, Michael's eyes went wide. He started toward her, then stopped.

'I can't let you,' he said. 'It's too dangerous.'

'I'll be safer in town actually,' Nisha said. 'You know I will.'

'On the way, though. The bridge. You can't do it.'

'I'm afraid of you. I'm more afraid of you than of the storm.'

You are the storm was what she wanted to say. *I thought my sister was the storm but now I understand she's not it at all.* She saw Michael's hands curl into fists. She stared at his hands until he jammed them into his pockets.

'At least hug me,' he said.

'I'll hug you tomorrow or whenever this is all over.' She did not know what she meant by *this*.

Michael stayed where he was, on the other side of the kitchen table. Nisha let herself out into the rain. When she glanced back, she saw he was right there, watching out the window. He looked destroyed, impossibly old.

In a few seconds, she was soaked. Her hood blew back, the rain rushed inside the collar of her coat and down into her boots, soaking her pants legs, even though the house blocked most of the wind off the river. Still, this wind drove her down the stairs, the crazy combined forces of gravity and wind, nearly knocking her into the flooded garden. She fought her way to the car, wrestled the door open. Finally she was inside. Quiet, relatively. Not dry. She started the car, backed out, waved up at Michael as was their custom, even though she couldn't see his form in the window.

Michael had been right about the bridge.

There was a smaller lower bridge before it, over the mouth of Dawson Creek where it flowed into the Neuse. You could fish from this bridge, you could even jump from it, though signs warned against such recklessness. Nisha had to steer hard to the right to keep from being blown into the cement guardrail. The road beyond, open to the river on one side and the creek on the other, had already begun to flood. She drove through slowly, as the public service announcements always advised, even though she could see the water wasn't very deep, had not joined the river's current. It was brackish, though, she reminded herself, the salt likely to make a mess of the car's undercarriage. She thought of Boston in winter, DOT trucks spewing salt. Michael always said the damage here was just the same as from salted roads.

Two hundred feet beyond, houses at the river's edge sheltered the road, took the brunt of the wind, their lawns absorbing the rising river, at least for now, until the saturation point. The driving was easier here. Nisha knew there was one more open stretch, just before China Grove, where Lana Turner had a summer home. She wondered if Lana ever rode out any hurricanes, watching the water rise in the big house on the bend. In Hurricane Irene, all these houses had been wrecked. Two of them actually traded decks that had washed out into the river and then washed back, slowly crossing paths, while the two sets of owners tracked their progress. Neck and neck like a horse race, they said later, when people could laugh a little about things like that.

Why was she thinking about this now? For comfort? Just drive, she told herself. Concentrate. The wind behind her as she passed the acre of soybeans a rogue developer once planned to flood in order to build a marina. That work was about to be done for him now. Across the road was the gate into a creek-front community planned in 2007 and abandoned the next year in the financial crisis. One house built and sold. She wondered if anyone lived there. What isolation. Terrifying right now.

She came to the right turn at Oriental Road. She could go straight, the long way around, and avoid the bridge. Nisha knew this was probably the wiser course, but she turned anyway, or the car turned itself. She felt a strange giving up, giving in, and at the same time a powerful desire. She wanted to know. She wanted to have crossed the bridge and survived.

The odd thing about Walnut Grove Marina, on the near side of the bridge, was that it was quiet – no lines singing against theirs masts in this wind – and almost empty. People had moved their boats deep into the smaller creeks, Green or

Blount's, their hurricane holes. They tied the boats between the largest, strongest trees on either shore, loosely, so when the water rose, the boat did too. Braver, more experienced – maybe more foolish? – owners stayed on the boats, literally rose out the storm, fighting their way out on deck to adjust the lines.

On the low end of the bridge, she knew she'd made a mistake, and she slowed the car, wondering if would be wiser to turn back, or to get out of the car and walk across. *How would that be smarter?* Her mother's voice asked.

'I'm in trouble, Mommy,' Nisha said aloud. 'I'm so sad. I don't know what I'm doing here.'

She inched the car forward. The wind seemed to rush down from the top of the bridge, pushing her backwards. And wind came at her from the east too, wind and rising tide driving the river toward the village. This doubled force was confusing, it seemed to confuse the car, as if the car were sentient, an animal. I'm going to flood the engine, Nisha thought. Well, that's ironic. You could still just back up, downhill, drive around, she told herself.

She locked her elbows to keep the steering wheel steady and continued the ascent. She wondered, almost absently, as if she were not in her body, if her arms would break. The wind pushed the car across the centre line and into the left bike lane. The left side mirror scraped along the concrete railing and folded inward. Why had she not though to do that in the first place? It seemed now as if she might slam into the concrete and then through it and fall into the river.

Then the gust died, and she didn't crash. The view from the top of the bridge was exhilarating, shocking, terrible. The river had already washed over the docks in the marina. A small sailboat, a 25-footer Nisha guessed, had broken loose from its starboard dock lines and nestled into the boat beside it, hulls grinding together with every wave that came in. An owner who lived out of town. Bad luck to berth next to an absentee. Water covered the parking lot and the first step of the condos. Those people would have a rough night. If they had stayed.

No lights on in the village. Nisha wondered how long the power had been out. Another whistling gust of wind hauled the car back against the railing. The side mirror broke off and blew away over the bridge. Nisha pulled the wheel right as hard as she could.

'Idiot,' she said. 'Mommy, I'm so stupid.' But she knew she would be all right. She was on the downward slope now. The dock master's office and the yacht club sheltered this side of the bridge from the wind, a little anyway.

Water lapped in the road at the corner of Main Street, maybe about a foot deep. Nisha thought she could make it, even though the tires would be completely underwater. She could feel the car begin to float, drifting left, over the kerb into the driveway between the bank and the veterinary clinic. And then, just as suddenly, the wheels caught, rolled forward. Here the road ran slightly uphill, just enough for traction.

Thirty feet ahead, there was almost no standing water. Nisha turned right onto Church Street, drove past the town hall. She could see flashlights inside, moving figures. Branches littered the gravel drive into her parking area. She worried that a tree might come down on her car and wondered if she should park in the street. Plenty of trees there too. She would take her chances. The car was insured. Seemed like this would fall under the category of Acts of God.

She looked at her phone. A text from Michael. She hadn't even heard it.

For the smallest fraction of a second, Nisha thought she ought to text Djuna.

Made it, she typed. *I'm fine.*

Thank goodness, came the reply, immediately, as if Michael had already typed the words. *I love you. I'm sorry. Be in touch. I will too.*

Fifteen seconds from the car, the wind and rain driving harder than when she'd left the river house, up the steps and under the portico, inside the apartment.

Inside, dry, cool, fuzzy grey storm light illuminated the windows, as if through thin drapery. No power. Nisha had two phone chargers – the small one would charge the phone once, the larger one was good for two, maybe three charges. After that she knew she could charge the phone in the car.

Right now, though, that main thing was to make it through landfall, probably in the next few hours. She checked the NOAA website: Ismene's eye had clocked south. Wilmington would take the direct hit.

Nisha knew the safest place away from the windows would be the bathroom, but she wanted to watch the sky, the tops of the trees, their shadows, see the branches snap off if that's what was going to happen. She pulled the cushions off the couch and made a bed on the floor of the galley kitchen, between the oven and the sink. Then she dragged the rocking chair halfway behind the tall counter. She sat and rocked and listened, scanned the sky.

She imagined the fury outside was Djuna, Djuna's rage at missing everything, the entire rest of her life. A dervish without religion or reason – weren't those opposites anyway? Djuna's rage and the Earth's one and the same. You stupid, selfish people. The same people who caused these storms and fires to be so fierce, those people had murdered Djuna, ignorant people, waving guns around, in love with power. Djuna *was* the storm. Not Michael. Michael was maybe a gust of wind. Djuna was the whole spinning williwaw.

Nisha imagined that somewhere Djuna was leading the life of her second namesake, Parvati. Not leading the life. Leading the death? She didn't know how to phrase it. Something about the next world. In the next world, Djuna was Parvati, who could be gentle or fierce, loving or enraged. Just like the teenager Djuna was. Absorbed by Parvati. Merged. Language was so useless sometimes. Djuna was *elsewhere*, she said, just in the next county from home, astride her tiger on Atlantic Beach. Dawon is the tiger's name. A gift from her father, the living version of the tiger necklace he presented her on her 7th birthday. Oh no, Djuna had said when she opened the package and clasped the necklace around her throat. Now the tiger is riding me.

A gunshot. No, a splintering. Then silence again, except for the wind. A tree, Nisha knew, had come down very close. Not a gunshot really. Oh, Djuna. Howling. Who is that? She wondered. Djuna or me or the wind?

Somewhere behind the storm or above it, the sun set and the full-on hurricane became only sound, a constant rushing, sometimes a keening punctuated by the crack and thump of branches breaking nearby. At midnight, Nisha opened the door and aimed the phone's flashlight into the yard. Water had reached almost halfway up the steps, probably two feet. That would be all right if it didn't go much higher. She wedged bath towels at the bottom of the door just in case.

Landfall, the town website reported. Good that their generator was still running. Wilmington is inundated, wrecked. Closer, though, people were being rescued from the roofs of houses in New Bern.

Nisha wasn't sure if she'd slept, or when. She texted Michael.
So far okay, he wrote. *What about you?*
Fine, she wrote.
Any damage?
I haven't been outside yet.

She ate an apple, a few pretzels. She drank warm seltzer. She didn't want to open the refrigerator – there wasn't much inside anyway. She thought about having a real drink – there was a bottle of Irish whiskey in the cabinet above the sink, but in the end, she was frightened of losing reflexes, attention, what little control she had. Trees could still come down – the two trees she could see outside the tall windows, their roots loosened by all the rain, would fall onto her end of the building. Already, there was a different open space in the early morning view: the tree across the parking lot, that must have been the splintering she'd heard – when? Was that yesterday? Yes. How many hours ago? She wasn't sure. Time moved oddly, swam as if waterlogged.

But now the briefest silence itself was a sound. Nisha listened carefully, for changes, breaks, modulations. She wondered if she'd developed some sort of odd seeing blindness, so acute was her hearing, so completely did she depend upon it. Silence always so cherished in this apartment. Some lines about *a fine and quiet place*. Maybe this is what Djuna heard now, how Djuna listened now. And so, in this sense, Nisha felt the storm was another way to be closer to Djuna, to understand Djuna's death. The storm was sitting shiva, the storm was a wake, the letting go of the body. But in elemental terms, the storm was the opposite of immolation. Water and wind would always be the ruin of a funeral pyre.

Nisha realized she wanted the storm to last forever.

On Sunday morning, the fifteenth of October, the wind started to ease. Nisha heard a car on Church Street, one car churning through floodwater, and then hours later it seemed, another. More vehicles splashed by in the afternoon, so many that she stopped counting. This storm will end, she told herself. *Is* ending. It has to. That's how it works. The town website reported that the police said in a few hours, it would be safe enough for residents to come back and check on their homes, their boats. She wondered how many people had left and how many stayed. Around 11 a.m., someone knocked, called her name. I'm here, Nisha called out, I'm fine. She stood up from the rocking chair and went to the door. When she opened it, no one was there.

She stepped out onto the porch. The storm was beginning to tire itself out, a toddler nearly over her tantrum. Debris had washed halfway up the steps – three more inches and there would have been water in the house. A branch from the crape myrtle lay along the top step, as if it had been a barrier. Heroic. Maybe an offering. She thought it was a beautiful artifact – in some unforeseeable future she might imagine it varnished into a Christmas decoration.

Rain still blew through the yard between the old school buildings. Tree branches and leaves covered both parking lots. Nisha wondered if it was safe to walk around out here – if the shingles, branches, entire trees, had stopped falling. Maybe if she kept away from all of that, walked in the middle of the street? She picked a path through the parking lot, past the tree fallen on the neighbour's garage, turned right on Factory Street, heading towards the river. Some houses seemed to have been moved off their foundations. Debris everywhere. Someone's shed had come loose and floated to the river's edge. Farther along, an uprooted oak tree blocked the storm-driven progress of fencing and potted plants and a twisted Adirondack chair.

The fishing pier was gone, reduced to broken spikes of pilings and half-submerged boards. Two blocks to the east, the storm surge had broken the concrete roadway into an ar- chipelago. The intersection of High Street was a beach, sand built up like a two-foot-tall speed bump. At the corner of Front Street, rip rap and boulders blocked the road. Nisha thought of the barricade scene in *Les Misérables*. All that stuff piled up and still no defence. The rain came now as a drizzle, the wind less of a shout. She did not see another person. The scene was post-apocalyptic. It wasn't hard to imagine she was the only human left on Earth.

This must be what my heart looks like, she thought.

Nisha retraced her path back to the apartment and picked up the urn, walked back through the ruin to the river. She stepped carefully across the scattered rip rap, along the new spit of rubble that had formed, as far into the river as she could go, to the place where, ten years ago, Michael walked into the water with Djuna riding on his shoulders, as if she were Parvati, riding on Dawon, her tiger. Djuna, above the dark element, fearless in her new life on the other side of the world. Nisha opened the mouth of the urn over the water and shook it. The last breath of storm found its way inside and lifted Djuna's ashes into the air, carrying them upward, south towards the opposite shore, down to the water's sur- face and then up again, a swirl, a somersault. The ashes glit- tered a little in the weak sunlight, like mica, like light on water, the flash of a message, too quick, then gone.

The Authors

CHRIS BOGLE is a writer and director. He was raised in the North-East of England and made his start as a runner on the *Harry Potter* films at Alnwick Castle. His short films have screened internationally at BAFTA recognised festivals and is an alumnus of the Edinburgh International and Reykjavik International Film Festival talent labs. He has an MA in filmmaking and is currently studying for a master's in Creative Writing. Chris' primary interest is in fiction and stories about people on the social and class margins. He has two young boys and enjoys surfing and living near the beach.

MEI DAVIS is a former Angeleno now living in the cold wilds of Metro Detroit. Sometimes she writes.

AOIFE ESMONDE is from Cork, now based in Dublin, with a background in academia, library work, and publishing. Aoife came to writing late but with enthusiasm, and is now working on a novel. This is Aoife's first short story.

KASANDRA FERGUSON is a writer, painter, and baker from the American Midwest currently studying Literature and Publishing at NUI Galway. Her greatest ambition is to be both and author and an editor at an independent press. She can often be found in a bookshop buying novels she doesn't actually have time to read.

HELENA PANTSIS (she/they) is a writer and bad artist from Naarm, Australia. A full-time student of creative writing, they have a fond appreciation for the gritty, the dark, and the experimental. Her works are published in *Overland*, *Island Online*, *Going Down Swinging*, and *Meanjin*. More can be found at hlnpnts.com.

SANDY PARSONS' fiction can
   be read in *Analog Science
   Fiction and Fact*, *Escape Pod*,
   and *Reckoning*, among others.
   In addition to writing fiction,
   Sandy also narrates audio fiction. When not
   writing, Sandy works as an anesthetist in Georgia.
   More information and links to stories can be
   found at sandyparsons.com/

JAMIE PERRAULT is a queer agender veterinarian living
   and working in the Midwest. They have twins, a wonderful
   genderqueer spouse, and four cats at home to help the writing.
   They have been published in *Apparition Literature*, the *Crow's
   Quill*, and several independent anthologies.
   They can be found on Twitter @awritinghope.

DANIEL RAY lives in Tennessee and spends most of his time
   either reading or writing. *Where the Sun Is Always Setting* is
   his first story to appear in print.

SAMUEL SKUSE is a short story writer and playwright from
   Devon. He has had work published through *East of the Web*,
   Horla, *Enchanted Forest* and *INK*. His monologue *Roadmap
   Window* was performed at the *Ignite New Writing Festival* in
   2021. He is currently reading for MSt Creative Writing
   at Oriel College, Oxford.

COURTNEY SMYTH is from Dublin. They are a writer of both
   short and long stories about people, places and things. They have
   previously been published in *Paper Lanterns Literary Journal*.

TESSA SWACKHAMMER is a writer specializing in work that
   is painfully present in its dreamlike absurdity. Her poetry and
   short fiction have appeared in places like *Sledgehammer Lit*,
   Fifth Wheel Press, *Elpis Pages*, *Small Leaf Press*, and more. She
   was also shortlisted for the *Plough Arts Poetry Prize in 2021*,
   and a finalist in the *New Millennium Writing Awards* in 2022.

LIZ ULIN was the winner of the *Fresh Voices Screenplay Competition*, and a finalist in *The Canadian Short Script Competition*, *The Canadian Authors Association Short Story Competition*, and *The Writers Union of Canada Short Prose Competition*. In addition, she has had several short stories adapted and produced at Montreal's Centaur Theatre. Her work has been published most recently in *Short Circuit*, *Flash Fiction Magazine*, *Ninth Letter*, and the feminist anthology *Broad Knowledge*.

BRIGITTE DE VALK won the *Cúirt New Writing Prize 2020* (adjudicated by Claire-Louise Bennett), and the *Royal Holloway Art Writing Competition*. She was awarded second place in the *Benedict Kiely Short Story Competition* and was longlisted for *The Alpine Fellowship Writing Prize 2020*. Her entry to the *Bournemouth Writing Prize 2021* was selected for publication. Brigitte's short fiction is also published by *Happy London Press* and *Reflex Press*.

HOLDEN WERTHEIMER-MEIER lives in Brooklyn, NY, USA with his wife. He holds a degree in Creative Writing from Knox College in Illinois, USA.

LIZA WIELAND has published nine books, most recently *Paris, 7 A.M.*, a novel about the poet Elizabeth Bishop in Paris in the 1930s. She is Professor Emerita of English at East Carolina University.